Angus MacDream

and the

Roktopus Rogue

To Barry Drucker

Isabelle Raney Freedman

April 2011

the **Snugglay Islands**
off the West Coast of Scotland

BLANKET BEACH

QUARTZ BEACH   White Sand   BOLSTER BAY   Black Sand

DROP-OFF CLIFFS   Impassable Jagged Rocks   Angus' House   DODO   Mangroid Trees

MacAllister's House   BEN SLUMBER   Deep Woods   VILLAGE OF NAP

LOCH SNOOZE   LITTLE "wee" SNUGGLAY

MEADOW   SLUMBER STRAIT

BEACHES

Angus MacDream
and the
Roktopus Rogue

By

ISABELLE ROONEY-FREEDMAN

ILLUSTRATIONS by TERI RIDER

A Word with You Press
Publishers and Purveyors of Fine Stories
802 S. Tremont St.
Oceanside, California 92054

This book was written for
Lincoln Graeme Freedman

Almost Avalon
by Thornton Sully
A young couple struggles with love and life on the island
frontier just twenty-six miles west of Los Angeles.

The Mason Key II: Aloft and Alow
by David Folz
Both battle and storm sends Mason to a deserted island where
survival leads to unexpected treasures.

Bounce
by Pulitzer Prize winner, Jonathan Freedman

A nutty watermelon, a spurned she-lawyer, a frustrated
Carioca journalist, and a misanthropic parrot set off to
Brazil to change the world.

A Word with You Press
Publishers and Purveyors of Fine Stories
802 S. Tremont St.
Oceanside, California 92054

Acknowledgments

This book has been a collaboration between myself, Teri Rider, and our generous and considerate editor and publisher Thorn Sully. The joy it has brought me was completely unexpected. I thank my husband, Jonathan, for unswerving belief and encouragement, and my children, Viva and Lincoln, who are my inspiration.

Contents

Angus MacDream
and the
Roktopus Rogue

Chapter One

The Ticket to Unimaginable Danger

Being given a grant to do field work for the Department of Defensive Operations on a tiny Scottish island that you've never heard of might just be a ticket to unimaginable danger. You'd think my parents would have thought of this when it happened to them, but they are advanced theoretical physicists and have their heads in the clouds.

"The Army wants to explore the particle-wave-particle nature of dreams?" I asked.

"That's right, Angus," my mom flicked her thick black braid over her shoulder. "Soldiers have dreams, don't they? So the Army needs to understand them. Right, hon? Danny?"

"Umm," my dad said, absently. He was patting himself all over, looking for his glasses or his pen. He wore a plaid shirt and jeans, which is more or less a uniform for advanced theoretical physicists. He does not have a beard, but his hair does stand up in blond spikes, which makes it look like the electrical activity in his brain is zapping through his head. Which I guess it is.

Delicately, my mom peeled a lettuce leaf off his salad plate, and there were the glasses. My dad's face brightened, and he waggled his hands with the joy of discovery.

I continued, "And we have to move to an island off the West Coast of Scotland because?"

"Well," she looked confused for a moment, and then said, "Because that's where the critical mass is."

"*Critical mass?*" I imagined a festering heap of some horribly explosive, probably radioactive substance.

"Of people. A critical mass is when you have the right number of the right people together in the same place working on an important question. All the cyberdream researchers worth the name will be on Little Snugglay this summer."

"Why can't they be in California?" My mom and dad both worked at UCSD.

"Because getting people together in a quiet remote location fosters intellectual excellence. You know, like when they did the Manhattan Project in Los Alamos."

"Where they invented the atomic bomb you mean? Didn't they do that in a remote location to protect people from the potentially devastating effects of a nuclear accident?"

My mother blinked. She was wearing a floppy blue garment, which at the moment was a long skirt. It could be a skirt, a medium length strapless dress, or a poncho, which was why she liked it. She started fidgeting with it, pulling it up over her purple T-shirt to make the dress. Later in the day, when the temperature fell, she would pull on jeans and the skirt-dress would enter the third stage of its life, as the poncho. My mom might look a little odd if she was not very, very pretty, but she is, so I guess she can wear what she likes. Her name is Julia.

She looked sideways at my dad, who was again patting himself for the glasses, which were now on the top of his head.

My mother pushed them down to his nose, and he did the hand-waggle again, as if he had just been blessed with the gift of sight. Which I guess he had.

"Whatever," said my mom. "There's no work like that being done on the Snugglays. Angus, are you worried about going to Scotland because of, you know, your first parents?"

That got my dad's full attention and he snapped his head round to look at me.

See I was born in Scotland, and my parents adopted me and brought me to California when I was a baby. My dads were brothers. My first dad died in a climbing accident right before I was born, and my first mom died in the hospital right after, so I don't remember anything about it. I have some pictures, and a diary that my first mom kept when she was pregnant with me. I can ask my mom and dad about my first mom and dad anytime I want, but I don't too often, because I don't want to hurt their feelings. I'm their only kid. They tried, but they couldn't have more. There's a genetic problem. Any kid they have would have a one-in-four chance of being really sick.

"No, Mom," I said, "That isn't it. Well, OK, it may be a little weird, but I have to face it sometime. I can't avoid a whole country for the rest of my life—not one I'm a citizen of, anyway."

"You know, we won't be anywhere near where...where you were born," said my mom. "We don't have to go there. I mean, unless you want to..."

"*Mom!* It's fine," I said. "Too much information, OK." I needed to make sense of my own feelings before I discussed this, so I changed the subject. "It's just—a whole summer away from the Pacific Ocean."

This was true. I am a surfer. That's a surfer of waves, not the net. I've been a surfer since I was four years old, and my dad put me in Menahune surf camp and bought me my first baby surfboard. When you grow up next to the Pacific, surfing is a way of life. I surf, my dad surfs, even my mom has been know to belly board a bit. They had bought me my first Quicksilver board for my twelfth birthday the month before. I couldn't stand to leave it idle all summer.

"Oh, you can surf Scotland," said my dad. He pushed some orange peel off his laptop and accessed a website called, appropriately enough, "Surfing Scotland." There was a movie of some kids and bearded old guys in wet suits, and I had to admit it did look reasonable, if a bit gray.

"Whoa!" I said, watching a kid surf a barrel, and I was getting amped against my better instincts. "Is that the Slumber Strait?"

"Well, no," said my dad, "that's the ocean off the island of Mull. You can't film on the Snugglays without a special license. But you can surf there."

No overcrowding then. It suited me.

I wouldn't give in too easily, though. "I'll miss the pelicans," I said, "and the seals. I was going to help out on that seal tracking project, remember?"

All my life I've wanted to work in the life sciences: marine biologist, if I can make the grades.

"Aha!" My dad starting tapping on his keyboard again. "The Hebrides are a nature-lover's paradise. One of the few unspoilt locations in the Western World."

Of course I knew the Scottish Islands were a bird sanctuary. But…

"Whoa!" I said again, at the creature on the screen. *Scorpohamster?* I had never seen anything like it. There was a picture of a yellow, furry, mouse-like creature with a long, wicked looking, greenish-black tail that had a spike on the end of it. I read:

The soft, furry bodies of these shy, inoffensive creatures are well defended by the crusted, black, venomous tail. Adult scorpohamsters are typically 6 cm (4 inches) in length, while the tail can easily reach 15 cm (10 inches) fully extended. The tail is carried rolled in a tight coil, but scorpohamster can unroll and extend it rapidly, and can whip it with great speed and extreme accuracy in all directions, facilitating delivery of venom with deadly precision. Supplies of an antidote to the venom are maintained at the DODO clinic on Great Snugglay, and at the Oban Infirmary.

"Whoa!" I said again. My parents looked at me, curiously. Nothing was really astonishing or exciting to them unless it was a wave-particle. Or something.

"How come I never heard of scorpohamster?" I demanded. "Why isn't that in the newspapers?"

"All of this is classified," my dad said. "You need a special password to access the site."

I looked again at the screen again. It said:

Department Of Defensive Operations (DODO) File
Wildlife of the Snugglay Islands
0001: *Scorpohamster*
Phylum: *ArthroChorda*

I was practically choking. "Why did you not tell me this before? These are new species? I'd get to study new species? At the age of 12?"

They looked at each other and shrugged. "Sure, sure," they said. Relieved that this was what it would take to get me to come quietly–or noisily but happy.

"There are more?" I almost squeaked.
My dad pushed the screen at me.

0002: *Roktopus*
Phylum: *Mollusca*

These shy, intelligent cephalopods have a body, with a central mouth and a hard beak, and eight tentacles. Adult male and female roktopi are typically 4 inches in diameter, but may grow to the size of a soccer ball, with tentacles that may be up to 1 meter (3 feet) long. There is no internal skeleton but in health the animals are completely covered with small rocks. Sodium carbonate and calcium chloride, secreted separately from ducts co-localized in the skin, react to form the calcium carbonate "rocks" which remain anchored to the ducts:

$$Na_2CO_3 + CaCL_2 = 2NaCl + CaCO_3$$

The calcium carbonate, which forms the rocks, is naturally white, but roktopus can add pigment to the ducts, providing the opportunity for camouflage. The classic purple and green coloration of wild roktopi allow them to blend easily with the bed of the Slumber Strait, which is rich in amethyst and chalcedony. Roktopi studied in captivity alter their coloration to match their new surroundings.

Roktopi do not surface often, due to buoyancy issues, and prefer to lie flat on the seabed, pretending to be a pile of small rocks. When threatened, they may spray a jet of rocks, which blinds and confuses the aggressor, while roktopus makes its escape. When more aggressively attacked, the animal may separate a tentacle or two, which, rich in nervous tissue, continues to crawl along the seabed, deflecting the predator's attention from the remainder of the roktopus.

If there is no alternative, as when babies are threatened, roktopus can be an enthusiastic fighter, whomping opponents with all eight rock-encrusted tentacles. The well-defended roktopus is rarely hurt in such encounters, but may have to hole up for a few days after battle to regrow dislodged rocks.

Like scorpohamsters, and most of the other creatures I read about that day, roktopi were shy and inoffensive, endangered, and strictly protected by law.

But there was nothing shy, inoffensive, endangered or small about the first roktopus I encountered. It was gigantic, it was angry, it was hungry for lunch, and its lunch had a name. The name of its lunch was Angus MacDream.

Chapter Two

Paralyzed, But Not Yet Eaten

It happened on our third day on Little Snugglay. At first, all three of us just lay around, feeling dizzy and sick. Part of it was jetlag, and part of it was the trip—by plane to New York, then to Glasgow, then to a village called Oban, then a rough ride on a DODO boat to the island—but I heard later that all the scientists and their families experienced several days of disorientation when they came here, even the ones from Europe, who had traveled only a few hundred miles.

My parents were still in bed with their door closed when I gulped down some OJ and splashed water on my face to wake up. It was 6 a.m. I needed to surf.

I'm not supposed to surf alone, especially since the accident last year when my fin hit my face and carved out a C-shaped curve under my left eye. For anyone who doesn't surf, your board is attached to your ankle by a leash. It helps you to not lose the board, but in an accident, you're more likely to be hit. I have a white scar, but it fits with the planes of my face, and when I am older it will look like an expression line. Anyway, on that occasion I was dazed, and if my friends had not helped me out I guess it might not have gone so well.

I knew my parents were right, but there was no way my dad was fit to surf with me—I'd heard him hurling during the night—and I didn't know anyone else to surf with yet. I was just going to go down to the beach and if it were mild I would bodysurf a few. Nothing extreme. If the surf were rough I'd just watch the waves and stay in the shallows. Get my feet wet, at least.

I pulled on shorts and sneakers and snuck out quietly, grabbing my wetsuit and the one board that I'd been able to bring on the plane, my Quicksilver, from the mudroom at the back of the cottage. There was no record of habitation on the Snugglays, but there were buildings—a whole village of stone cottages that the DODO had moved into and fixed up, so people must have lived here at one time. It was called The Village of Nap. There were local people here now as well, but they had come across from other islands, attracted by the jobs that the DODO community was creating, and they had all signed the Defensive Secrets Act.

I ran the few hundred yards to the beach, which was grayish white and rough; not fine sand, but larger particles that you could see were fragments of shells, and little rocks, yellow and purple and pink mixed in with the gray and white. I'd heard that the surf was good off the West Coast of these islands, nothing to break the waves for endless miles, until you hit the East Coast of the USA, and they hadn't been kidding. The surf was regular and clean, not too high today, not rough, with a predictable rhythm—6 small waves and a big one, 6 small waves and a big one. Beach breaks. White capped and perfectly formed, maybe eight feet high, so very safe. Couldn't have asked for better. The smell of the sea and the wind off the ocean cleared my head and I was amped. I pulled my suit on impatiently, then grabbed my board and ran down to the water, feeling the particles crunch under my bare feet. The water was cool, but not freezing—like the Pacific in early spring. I paddled out and waited for one of the breakers.

My wave did not disappoint. I caught it easily, straightened my arms and scooped my legs under my body so I was standing on the deck, balanced, heading for shore, fast and smooth. Not that I'm the world's greatest surfer, by a mile or more, but these waves were a gift.

I hopped off in the shallows and immediately paddled out for another wave. Same deal. I couldn't believe I had this place to myself. There must be other surfers on the island, but it was early, and there were other beaches, too. I'd hook up with some buddies eventually.

On the crest of my third wave, I felt something grab at my board, then slip off, like I'd surfed through a big frond of seaweed. I was startled, and rocked a bit, but stayed up, then caught my breath in the shallows.

I looked out at the ocean. I wasn't worried. There were no dangerous animals here. You might see a basking shark, which were huge, but harmless, and there were none of the big, bad, biting kind. The only possible dangers in the water were the little roktopi, which can bite and spray you with a relative of tetrodotoxin. This is what they use to paralyze their prey, but they only attack larger animals if threatened, and it would take five or six of them to stop a person of my size breathing, and anyway, I'd read that they're never found in open water, but stay in the shelter of the Slumber Strait, between the islands. I decided to go out again.

My fourth wave was a different story. I was up, on a high crest, a bit higher than the last ones, I thought, when something slapped my board hard. I looked down, and there was a section of something long and rubbery, but crusted with purple and green lumps, draped over the front of the board, and slithering off. I watched it disappear back into the ocean, and saw the tapered tip flip up, like waving goodbye. There were suckers on the underside. It couldn't have taken more than a second, but I had time to ask myself, *some weird kind of kelp?* when it suddenly pointed out of the water and slapped the Quicksilver again, then wrapped around it. I felt a tug and realized there was one wrapping around the back of the board as well. The board was pulled away from me, dragged under the white cap, and for an awesome moment I was standing on the wave.

Then another lumpy green and purple frond slicked out of the ocean and grabbed me. It curled around my chest and started to squeeze, and another one had my thighs. I sucked a great gulp of air before they pulled me under.

The world under the water was green, silent and frantic. At first I couldn't make anything out through the foam, but I felt the rubbery muscle of the thing that was crushing me. If there had been anything worth breathing under the ocean I wouldn't have been able to breathe it. As I was pulled down deeper, the water cleared, and I saw what it was. Roktopus! But not any kind of roktopus I'd read about. This was a monster. Its body was roughly spherical, eight or nine feet in diameter. Each blue eye was the size of a beach ball, and the two tentacles that grabbed me were each wrapped three times around my body, with length to spare. Other tentacles waved around excitedly. It was covered all over with sharp, knobby, green and purple rocks, some the size of a marble, some the size of baseballs. Worst of all was the vicious looking, razor-sharp beak in the centre of its body, big enough to eat me in a couple of bites, that the tentacles were pulling me towards.

My arms were free, and I dragged at the tentacle that was crushing my chest with all the strength I had. It was like trying to bend steel. I dug my fingers under the top loop, thinking that the underside might be sensitive enough to hurt, or at least irritate, and gouged at it with my nails. Something came away. Rocks. Green and purple rocks. The flesh beneath was smooth, rubbery, solid muscle. It was like fighting an anaconda. Through the pain in my chest, and the air hunger, I realized that at twelve years old I was going to die here, and I saw my mother's face, grief-stricken. It had been a good life, but way too short. My face took a harder, sharper bump as the Quicksilver butted my cheekbone, then floated away. I realized that the leash had broken, which was probably a good thing, but I'd likely never see that board again in one piece. This made me angry—which probably saved my life. As the tentacles pulled me within striking distance of the beak, and the beak opened and reached to rip my head off, I punched the monster in the eye.

It let go of me, and its tentacles thrashed. It spat something black that fouled the water, and I tasted bitterness mixed in with the salt. *Toxin*, I thought, *the good times just keep coming.* Green and purple rocks pelted me as I floated up. Through the surface of the water I saw the Scottish sun, blue sky with a few clouds scudding, a perfect day. I blacked out before I could breathe any of it in.

When I woke I was lying face up on the gritty beach, feeling like the ocean had spat me out because I tasted nasty. I coughed, and salt water trickled out of my mouth, then more fluid—it was my own saliva, which probably meant I was going to throw up. *Turn over,* I thought. My arms and legs flapped like beached fish, but I couldn't control them. My lips and tongue felt rubbery, my head was dizzy and sore. Well, severe muscular exertion and terror will do all those things to you, but this was worse than that—the roktopus had poisoned me. I was still breathing, but for how long?

Controlling the panic, I ran through what I knew about roktopus toxin. There were no reports of poisoning in humans, but it was a relative of the tetrodotoxin that's produced by the blue-ringed octopus and puffer fish, and it acted in more or less the same way, although it was more dilute and less potent—at least to crabs. It blocked sodium channels and induced muscle paralysis, which usually kicked in after thirty minutes. I had no idea how long I'd been out, so couldn't say if my symptoms were faster or slower than usual. The symptoms usually started with tingling and numbness of the tongue and lips *(check)*, and then more generalized paraesthesia (that's pins and needles to you, *check*). Then there was lightheadedness *(check)*, drooling and sweating *(check)* and paralysis of the arms and legs *(getting there)*. Eventually, the muscles of respiration failed and you suffocated, which was somewhat ironic after being crushed and almost drowning. Oh yeah, your thinking remained clear and you stayed conscious until you had brain damage. *Excellent.*

If you survived for twenty-four hours, you recovered, but the way things were going, that wasn't in my future. It might take six average size animals to seriously affect me, but Rocky-of-the-Sea had pumped enough bad juice to take out the Padres and the Chargers combined.

Another detail: there was an antidote to roktopus toxin—not that it was going to help me. The beach, as I had been congratulating myself a short time earlier, was deserted. I tried yelling, and made some wounded sounds that were snatched by the surf and carried out to sea. My head flopped to the side, and I saw a piece of the broken Quicksilver sticking up in the shale, like the fin of some buried sea creature. I tried using all my concentration to dig my heels and push myself backwards, and I did move a few pathetic, waggling inches. OK, pathetic or not, if I was going out I was going out fighting. I dug my heels again.

I heard something that might have been voices, but couldn't turn my head to look. I stopped my stupid shuffle up the beach, and put my energy into yelling. I managed the wounded animal howl again, and then heard the voices, closer.

"I think he's hurt, Mum!"

And then, feet pounding on the crunchy beach.

A face leaned over me; it was white, with freckles, blue eyes, and curly red hair.

"Y'awright, Chief?" It had a Scottish accent, and looked about twelve, same as me.

I blew bubbles through the drool running over my rubbery lips, and said something like, "Ambla bambla!"

Another face joined the first one. This one had red hair and blue eyes also, and was very pretty (though I think my mom is actually better looking).

"I don't think he can talk, Mum," the first face said.

"Are you hurt, son? What happened to you?" the mum face said.

"Ambla blub blub!"

"Looks like a surfing accident," the first face said. "He's really banged up, but looks like he's been pelted with rocks."

"Ambla! Blub!"

"You *have* been pelted with rocks? You feel like you've been pelted with rocks?"

"Son," said the mum face urgently, "can you feel your feet? Can you move them?"

"Bubbla, bubbla!" With a huge effort, I waggled my hands and feet, and then began to shake uncontrollably.

"Well, his neck's not broken," said the mum. "He's conscious, and understands us. He's drooling," she touched my forehead, "and sweating, trembling and poor muscle control. It looks for all the world like…Son, did something bite you? Or spit at you?"

"Ambla! Olbapop!"

"A roktopus?"

"Arr! Olbapop!"

"There's no roktopi in the open ocean," said the boy.

"Shut up, Malcolm. Are you sure, son?"

"Ambla!"

"Listen to me. You have to be sure. I have the antidote, but I have to be certain before I give it to you."

"Ambla! Olbabop!" My "words" were slurring more now, and I needed all my strength to get air in.

"Mum, you can't!"

"I'm giving it to him!" she said. "Cut his sleeve off, Malcolm!"

So she was a doctor and she had a doctor bag, which just happened to contain the medicine I needed to save me from certain death. I was being rescued by a team of medical beachcombers. If I hadn't just been crushed, beaten and poisoned by a gigantic, eight-tentacled, rock-encrusted, homicidal mollusk, I would have felt very lucky indeed.

They rummaged in their drybag, and then her hands came into view, tapping a syringe full of clear liquid.

"I'll have to calculate the dose," she said. "Would you say he's about 120 pounds?" I felt cold, surgical steel against my arm, and knew that Malcolm was cutting my sleeve off with scissors.

"If you're wrong, Mum, you could lose your medical license."

"Shut up, Malcolm!" she said.

Shut up, Malcolm! I thought.

Then the needle slid into my vein.

But breathing was getting harder and harder.

"Son, I'm going to put a tube in your throat, and we'll breathe for you. You'll be fine. Eventually."

"Assuming you didn't give him too much and he's not allergic."

"Shut up, Malcolm."

She pushed something plastic down my throat and attached a bag to it. I felt sweet, precious air flood my chest.

"Take over, Malcolm," she said. "Bag him."

"Aye, awright. How long for do we do this?"

"Until he can breath on his own. Could be a few hours. Hang on, I'm calling for help."

"You'll be lucky. Cell phones work here about fifty percent of the time," Malcolm's face informed me. "This close to the ocean, maybe twenty percent."

"I got through!" she announced, triumphantly. "We need a medical vehicle. Blanket Beach."

"Why they call this one Blanket is a mystery to me," said Malcolm, in a conversational tone, still bagging. "It's the scratchiest beach I've ever seen. There are soft sand beaches here as well, but..."

"Unnh!" I managed around the airway.

"Y'awright, Chief?" he said, kindly.

As I mentioned, he looked about twelve, but had clearly done this before, and was used to working with his mother. Through the pain and relief, I began to wonder what the setup was.

"They're coming," his mother said. "How you doing, son? How you doing, Malcolm?"

She went into her drybag again, and I felt her gentle hands wiping my face. When she lifted the gauze away it was red. Not just sweat, then. Those rocks had done some damage. Now that I knew what was happening to me, and was no longer fighting for air, I began to take stock of my body. Every part of it hurt, but I didn't think the damage was too serious. I might have broken a rib or three, but obviously my lungs were working.

"No pneumothorax," said the mum, confirming this. "Just relax."

I relaxed. Malcolm bagged. Malcolm and his mother talked to me quietly, keeping my mind occupied, while the mother took my pulse, felt my head, watching, I realized, for signs of allergic reaction.

"We've tested this antidote on human volunteers—and animals, of course—but you're our first subject in the field."

Wow! I was honored.

"We'll write it up, Malcolm," she continued brightly, "and you'll get your name on the paper."

"Magic!" Malcolm said, and bagged more enthusiastically.

While he bagged, and she monitored, they told me all about themselves. Her name was Maggie MacDodd and she was a doctor and biochemist—part of a team investigating the toxic and medicinal properties of the many new animal and plant species that were indigenous to the Snugglays. Malcolm, as I had guessed, was twelve. She was one of the medics on emergency call, which was why she carried the kit with the airway and the antidote, although she had never expected to use it because, she explained, it would take six angry roktopi to stop a person my size from breathing, and it takes a lot of aggression to annoy six roktopi that much.

"I think he was swimming in the Strait," said Malcolm. "Maybe disturbing their eggs, or something, and they ganged up on him. That's the only thing that would rattle them enough. Then he walked over here to surf, not knowing he'd been poisoned. Then, he fell off his board and got washed up. Probably scratched his face and hands trying to crawl up the beach."

"Is that what happened?" asked his mother.

"Unnh!" I telegraphed all the indignation I could manage, which isn't easy when you can't move your face.

"See, there are no roktopi in the open sea," Malcolm said, reasonably.

"Unnh!"

I coughed, I gagged, I spat. I don't know if the need to be understood did it, but power was returning.

"He's trying to breath on his own!"

My abilities came back quickly. I reached up and pulled the airway out. Then sucked great gulps of air in by myself. Within a few minutes, I could move everything.

"Whoa!" Maggie said. "There's no way you can recover that fast! No, don't sit up!"

I sat up. Pain blasted through my body. I lay down again.

"Was a giant roktopus," I gasped.

"No, there *are* no giant roktopi."

"Was thirty feet long."

"Not."

"Eyes like beach balls."

"No way, Chief."

"Broke my *surfboard!*"

They looked at each other significantly, clearly disbelieving.

"Don't try to talk," Maggie said soothingly. "It is true that there might still be something that big that we don't know about. If there's a monster in the ocean, the DODO will find it."

Further argument was stopped by the arrival of the medical vehicle, which drove me to the clinic in the DODO compound.

When my parents showed up, and I saw my mother's face, I wanted to hurl. She slumped against my dad and he held her up. My dad's face wasn't too hot, either.

See my parents have no fear for themselves. I think they see death as an intriguing scientific proposition—a new and exciting kind of wave-particle-hood. But if they think I might get hurt or die, or something, they're like scared little kids.

At this point all they had been told that I was in the hospital, had been found on the beach, and wasn't badly hurt.

So they were mainly upset about what might have happened, and, I guess, what might still happen on a day when I wasn't so lucky. It was impossible to explain why I had done it.

"I needed to surf," I said, lamely.

There was no shouting, no hand waving, no *what were you using for brains?* All of that would come later. Right then I wouldn't have minded if they grounded me for the rest of my life. Heck, I was thinking of grounding myself for the rest of my life.

"Your face looks like a hamburger with eyes," said my dad. My mom started to cry.

When they heard about the roktopus, the paralysis, the miraculous rescue, they raised a storm with the DODO, who banned all water sports for two weeks while they searched for major sea creatures. This really endeared me to the islands' teenage population, especially when they didn't find anything.

Another wrinkle—there was no trace of roktopus toxin or its known breakdown products in my bloodstream. Now, what with me being the first human to be poisoned by a roktopus (yay!) no one knew how the human body dealt with the poison. Maggie said it was entirely possible that they just didn't know what metabolite to look for. But the seed of suspicion was sown.

Other things that cast doubt on my story: there were no signs of the green and purple rocks that I claimed had torn my face up and, although there was some bruising on my upper body, it was consistent with me having a fight with my surfboard and then being dumped on the beach. There was nothing to finger a giant, rocky tentacle.

And finally, the kicker—*I had been surfing alone off a deserted, unfamiliar beach when I had been told not to, which was not only stupid, but wrong.*

To summit, I was the classic unreliable witness.

They more or less accepted that I hadn't been messing with the Slumber Strait, but only because there was no evidence of disruption there.

Which left the question of what *had* caused my paralysis? I heard one of the doctors ask my parents if I had any history of "emotional problems" and they denied it, furiously, but I could see that they were worried as well.

In the end, they decided that I had been attacked by seaweed while surfing illicitly, then got tangled and banged up in a struggle with the seaweed and my board, which got smashed in the process, then got washed up, half drowned and unconscious, and my imagination took care of the rest.

The worst of it was that Malcolm's mom took some heat for administering a still experimental antidote to a minor child who had not, in fact, been poisoned. She was not in really bad trouble, or on probation, because nobody really knew what had happened, and she had acted on the best information she had. It was more like other doctors making mean doctor jokes behind her back, and a small cloud was following her around. Like she wasn't being fired, but she might be passed over for promotion next time. That was enough to make me feel lousy, but she was cool about it. She said she still believed that I had been poisoned by something and that the antidote had saved my life, but she just couldn't prove it.

I started looking for ways to make it up to her.

To tell you the truth, by the end of the next day, when my face was scabby instead of raw, and I needed to surf again, but couldn't ask Mom and Dad for another board until there had been at least another week or two of "talks," I was beginning to doubt my story myself.

Still, it was because of my encounter with that roktopus that I was less surprised than I might have been otherwise when the seal climbed out of the water and turned into a girl...

Chapter Three

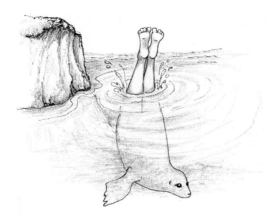

When the Seal Climbed Out of the Water and Turned Into a Girl

She did this in Bolster Bay, which is a natural, C-shaped inlet with rocky, pebbly sides curving around a white sand beach. Malcolm and I were down there photographing scrabs with his digital camera, Malcolm's dad, Rory MacDodd, was Head of Information Technology for the DODO site, which meant that he kept all the computer networks running and made sure people got their emails. The DODO had built two WIFI towers, one on each of the two Snugglay Islands, and all communication with the outside world depended on them and Malcolm's dad. He could get state of the art equipment super cheap, and knew how to run all the apps for it.

Malcolm was becoming my best friend on the Snugglays, which was lucky because I already had a bad rep with the other kids on the islands, first for having hysterical paralysis in response to a seaweed attack, and second for getting them banned from the water while the DODO checked out my hokey story.

The scrabs were out in big numbers, foraging around in the rock pools for the little shrimps and fish that they ate.

"It's called a *scrabble of scrabs*," Malcolm said.

Predictably, I had never seen anything like them before. They were about three inches long, top to tail, bright, hard, shiny and green. They looked like the back end of a beetle stuck to the front end of a crab, they had twelve legs, and reminded me a bit of centipedes when they ran. Two fearsome pincers stuck out of the front of their heads, between them was a wide, horny mouth, and above that waved two big, round, googley eyes on stalks. Their bodies were shaped like cellos, with a waist between the front six legs and the back ones, and the abdomen ended in a long, black stinger. Malcolm said their venom contained a protein that built donut shaped holes in your blood cells, which let too much water in and made them explode, but they only used it for self-defense.

"Random," I remarked, standing well back.

"A sting from one of these wouldn't hurt you even as much as an ant bite," Malcolm said. "Think of them as big, gentle, flightless bees."

Some of them were green all over, others spotted with raised white circles—bubbles, really—these were the females.

"Those are baby cases," Malcolm said.

"*Baby cases?*"

"Their ovary is a thin layer under the shell. The eggs pop straight up into the bubbles, and the babies develop in there. When they're big enough, they can roll the bubble skin back, crawl around a bit, with their mums watching, and then crawl back in again for protection. These ones are all pregnant, but the babies aren't ready to come out, yet."

"Wow," I said. Roktopus or not, I couldn't believe how I'd lucked out. I'd seen more amazing things in the past month than in the first twelve years of my life.

"At least they're all arthropod," I observed, thinking of scorpohamster, which needed a whole phylum for itself.

"Look at that seal!"

It was a typical, sleek gray harbor seal, with big black eyes and whiskers.

"Owp! Owp!" it barked, as it flippered its way up the beach.

We could see just its head behind a big rock.

The gray skin split down the middle, and fell away on both sides from a face that was framed in long black ringlets.

"Oh man," I commented.

The rest of her came into the open, pushing her feet into sandals. She wore a silvery cotton sundress and was pulling on a gray hooded sweatshirt. In addition to the black curls, which she fluffed with her fingers, she had very white skin and eyes that were dark blue or black, depending. She might have been the prettiest girl I'd ever seen.

OK, OK. She was the prettiest girl I'd ever seen.

"Whoa!" I said softly. "Jings!" Malcolm said.

"What's your problem?" She had an island accent.

I looked at Malcolm, then back at the girl.

"We thought you were a seal."

"I am a seal." She tossed her damp ringlets. "To be precise, I'm a Selkie. Never heard of us, then?"

"No way!" Malcolm whispered.

"I love it when people argue about what species I am, when I've already made it clear," she said. "It's even better than when they argue about how I should pronounce my name, which, if you're interested, is Varry—spelt M.H.A.I.R.I.E.— Varry. It's Gaelic."

"Varry," I repeated, obediently.

"And it's obvious that you're an American." She said this as though being an American on the Snugglays was stranger than being a Selkie. Which I guess it was.

"Southern California," I supplied, helpfully.

She shrugged. "What broke your face?"

"I was attacked by a giant roktopus."

I could feel Malcolm rolling his eyes at this, but this girl—seal—was giving me back faith in my memory, and I figured she would have to be sympathetic.

"Right, I heard about you. Anxious Angus. See there *are* no giant homicidal roktopi."

"It was forty feet long!"

"Not. I've been swimming these waters for twelve years and I am not the only Selkie. If there was a giant roktopus, believe me, we would know." She stuck her chin out, daring me to disagree with this logic.

Malcolm jerked out of his stupor. "The scrabs are eating your skin!"

She had left it on the pebbles like a gray velvet wrap. Now it was covered with bright green, scuttling scrabs that were tearing holes in it with their pincers. Some of the babies, further developed than Malcolm had thought, had pushed their white canopies back and ventured out to partake of what was clearly a delicacy for scrabs.

Malcolm and I ran to it and started prizing the arthropods off and throwing them into the ocean, trying not to make the damage any worse.

She sat on a low rock and examined her fingers. "Broke a nail," she informed us, sounding bored.

We looked at each other, then at her.

So it turned out that she was able to change from seal to girl and back again, with or without water, and the ancient legend, that whoever steals a Selkie's skin has power over her, was total garbage. The skins were disposable and simply regrown. Yes, she had a high calorie requirement and didn't like too much sun.

"But we'd never keep an old skin and put it back on again. Yuck! I mean, what kind of biological sense would *that* make?"

Any ideas I'd had about what made biological sense had been whipped, crushed and poisoned by a mega-mollusc, sloughed off with a Selkie skin, and what was left was being diligently shredded by scuttling green babies from back bubbles. I tried to roll with the punches.

We watched the creatures devouring Mhairie's skin while we told each other about ourselves. She and her mother, brothers and sisters had lived on the island of Benbecula, but moved to Little Snugglay—otherwise known as "Wee Snugglay" to the natives—like many other Hebrideans, when the DODO arrived bringing jobs. They ran the café in the village of Nap, which was where our cottage was. Her mother was a Selkie too. She didn't mention a father, and we didn't ask.

Malcolm told her he was going to be a biophysical engineer, by which he meant a person who could make prosthetic arms and legs that you could actually move with your mind, and he might decide to start with a medical degree because it was good basic training and because, in bad economic times when research funding might be low, "people will always need doctors."

His mother and dad had permanent jobs with the DODO, so he would be living here year round and going to the free school that the DODO was setting up on Great Snugglay.

Mhairie said that she would be going there too, so they would be classmates. The school, which would have guest courses taught by the numerous different kinds of DODO scientists, as well as exposure to multiple languages and cultures, was a huge opportunity for Hebridean children.

Malcolm's face went pink at the news that he would be going to school with her, probably for years, whereas I might well be gone in a few short months. Now over the initial shock, he was bursting with curiosity about her, and I prayed that he could control himself until we knew her a little better. This was not the kind of princess you risked offending with personal questions like, "*So what happens when you take a shower?*" or, "*Do you eat live fish?*"

To discourage these kinds of inquiries, I jumped right in with News About Me. It was surprisingly easy and amazingly good to fill my new friends in on my hopes and fears.

I explained that my parents, Julia and Danny MacDream, are the kind of people who spend most of their lives thinking and talking fast and scribbling weird symbols. Once in a while, they come up with a complete theory, and do an experiment to test it out. The experiment costs millions of dollars and needs computers and magnets the size of hotels, which have to be built underground. If the experiment doesn't give them the result they expect, they propose the existence of a new wave-particle to explain that. They give the wave-particle a cool name, like Schadenfreude or Charisma, and a couple years later they win a Nobel Prize for this. (Note to file: you can always tell the inner circle scientists, because they talk about *a* Nobel Prize, not *the* Nobel Prize, as is said by lesser mortals).

My parents are widely expected to win *a* Nobel Prize when they prove the existence of the dreamon, by getting an experiment not to work properly. They just have to figure out the right experiment, which, eventually, they will. I mean they have the cool name already, so how hard could it be?

Although they are so smart, it took them a long time to figure out that I am not as smart as they are, but I think they get it now. They stopped trying to get me to think up cool names for wave-particles when I was about five, and for my eighth birthday they got me a membership of the World Wildlife Fund and adopted a Blue-Footed Booby in my name. They also try to be kinder when they talk about "Wet Science," although they still make it sound like changing a diaper.

Malcolm laughed when I told that part. Mhairie just rolled her eyes and drew circles with her toes in the sand.

The bottom line: nobody is going to give me a Nobel Prize for explaining why my experiment didn't work. I am going to have to roll my sleeves up and do experiments that involve pouring and mixing, things changing color, fluorescent tags and polyacrylamide gels, and that do work according to already established scientific principles.

Turns out, my biology teacher thinks I have a reasonable shot at making a go of this—and I am pretty stoked about that—but my parents still try to make me feel better about it sometimes.

Like the other day, my dad said, as though it was big news, "You know, if Alexander Fleming had not discovered penicillin, millions of fruitful lives would have ended early, most of them children which would really have been bad."

"Right," my mom agreed. "If Einstein had died of, say, an ear infection when he was two, we wouldn't have that theory of his which, whatever you think of it, did start up an essential discussion"

My mom and dad think Einstein's *Special Theory of Relativity* is something you should know about, but not take too seriously, like an airline flight schedule.

"And," my dad continued, "Fleming did it by the rules. He saw that mold growing on his agar plate was killing his bacterial colonies and hypothesized that the mold must contain an antibiotic. Serendipity. Observation, hypothesis, experiment. He ticked them off on his fingers. Observation *before* hypothesis. In this case, it got a result!"

They both looked at me, expectantly.

"Wow," I said. "Those are really insightful comments."

They grinned, and went back to their online string plasma argument.

"Between you and me," I confided to Malcolm and Mhairie, "it's lucky they adopted me rather than having a baby the regular way. I keep them grounded and connected to real life. I am their only permanent relationship with someone who is not stratospherically bright."

"If my mom ever gave birth," I told my new friends, "the resulting supergenius would be too out there to fit in with the rest of the human race. He could do untold damage, including to himself. I mean, unless the little guy had someone like me around to keep him straight."

Mhairie and Malcolm listened non-judgmentally. It's an unusual problem, genius parents (though not, I guess, on the Snugglays).

There was a change in the weather. The light dropped, like a dimmer had been turned, and a circular wind replaced the breeze off the ocean.

They crawled out from behind and under rocks. They were livid green with eyestalks bobbing and pincers waving. Scrabs. But not the kind we'd come to know and love.

These had bodies three feet long, each pincer was another foot, and the abdomen ended in a ten-inch black stinger. On their skinny, black jointed legs they stood eighteen inches tall, and they came forward like the dry rush of a brush fire.

They were all female, meaning that they all carried a private army on their backs. Ten to fifteen white bubbles, each of which snapped sharply open, revealing a full load of alert and hungry babies, all with claws snapping eagerly.

There were six of them, which meant two for each of us. Except that all of them wanted me.

Running was not an option.

The first was on me before I had time to react. As I jumped up off my rock, she laced her legs around my thighs and began to slither up my body, pincers snapping for my face and neck.

It was a good thing that Malcolm thought and acted quickly. He grabbed both of her eyestalks and pulled them hard.

The eyes came off in his hands, and he stood there for a minute, staring at them with his mouth hanging open while green jelly bubbled out of the stalks.

The scrab screamed, "Scree! Scree!" Her pincers snapped wildly and she loosened her grip. Malcolm dropped the eyes and pulled her off me. Her babies jumped ship and some scrambled under my shirt, nipping and snipping, while their mother lay shrieking and snapping on the sand. They were too small to do much damage, but the pinches hurt like heck. Warm trickles of blood ran over my chest. I admit I panicked, and batted frantically, to keep them out of my pants.

A few feet away from us, Mhairie was thinking fast as well. She picked up a fifty-pound rock and smashed it down on the nearest scrab, where the head joined the body. The scrab was pinned to the beach, eyestalks and pincers waving furiously in front of the rock, twelve legs scrabbling behind, while the stinger stabbed the sand. The bubble covers on her back were all open and her babies came cascading out, just as crazy for blood as their parent.

Help came from an unexpected source. A scrabble of regular scrabs, which were about the same size as the vicious infants, pattered over to engage them in mortal combat. They were evenly matched, but there were more of the normal adults. The babies were buried in a seething pile of green bodies, with occasional legs and eyestalks tossed into the air.

I peeled the last two little scrabs out from under my shirt and threw them, hard, onto the rocks. There were four more monster adults. The rest of the regular scrabs were taking care of one of them. She lay struggling on the beach, completely overwhelmed by hundreds of her smaller relatives. They had flipped her onto her back, clearly a compromising position for scrabs. Her twelve legs jiggled, trying to shake off the dozen or so creatures that clung to each of them, her stinger poked the air futilely, her pincers slashed at nothing, her eyes on their stalks rolled uselessly on the sand.

That left three.

Mhairie ran over to stand with Malcolm and me, and together we faced the advancing enemy. These three ran together and, as if they'd learned from their sisters' problems, they pulled their eyes in close to their heads, protecting them from grabbing hands.

We faced nine deadly weapons—six pincers and three stingers—any one of which could deal us certain death. There were also the bubble babies, under wraps and waiting for their moment. They were little, but I figured if you were stung by enough of them, you'd probably die. In pain.

We realized at the same time that we couldn't let them near us. One snap on one neck from one pincer, and one carotid artery would be pumping blood to a beach instead of a brain. One stab from one stinger, and all of our red cells would pop like balloons. Without looking away from them, we picked up hefty rocks, and braced for attack.

All three of them jumped for me at once. In that instant, I could see their jaws, with fangs, salivating. Had they had fangs before?

We threw our rocks with all the force we had and scored three direct hits to three underbellies. They were carried backwards, and smashed on the beach.

An instant of silence, then they scrambled up and jumped at me again.

We threw more rocks. They smashed on the beach. They got up again. And they jumped.

"Any ideas?" panted Malcolm, mid-throw.

The scrabs were not being damaged by the rocks. It was clear what was going to happen. We could only throw rocks for so long. We would run out of energy; we would run out of rocks; and then they would get us. Basically, we had run out of luck.

"You go!" I shouted. "They only want me!"

"No way!" my friends yelled together.

"Go!"

Over the sound of the surf, above us, the air filled with a noise like carpets being whacked rhythmically against a wall, and deep cries, "Cacaw! Cacaw!"

I looked up quickly between rock flings. Two enormous birds were swooping down on us. Reagles, the islands' top predator.

Their bodies were the size of Harley Davidsons, covered in green and purple feathers. Their wingspan was easily twelve feet. Their beaks were golden, wickedly sharp, and their black, bead-like eyes glittered with intelligence beneath a circlet, like a crown, of fearsome-looking golden spikes. Their huge claws were tensed open, ready to slash and grab, as they arrowed down on us.

Oh, man.

"Been good to know you both," Malcolm said.

"Nice fight, boys," admitted Mhairie.

"Go!" I tried one last time.

The reagles did not attack us; they went for the scrabs.

My hair blew in the warm breeze off their muscular wings; I saw their beaks open in a triumphant, "Cacaw!" as they each sank their claws into the brilliant green carapace of a scrab. Their talons crunched through the hard shiny chiton, and the arthropods shrieked in pain and fury.

The reagles lifted off, each now clutching a struggling scrab, while black ichor dripped from the wounds to sizzle on the sand. The birds hovered for a moment, looked straight at me, and cacawed once more before they soared up, over the distant cliffs, and out of sight.

A few dislodged babies fell and scuttled around our feet, squealing and looking for something to sting; we kicked them away. There was one adult left. She jumped. We pounded her with rocks. Malcolm ran behind and slammed a boulder down on her stinger. Furious, she twisted and the stinger broke away from her body.

"Stay behind it! Away from the claws!" Mhairie shouted.

She grabbed a back leg and Malcolm grabbed the other. While the beast waggled its pincers at me, they pulled in different directions. The legs snapped off. I leapt back as the front end lurched towards me.

My friends each grabbed the next leg up. Snap! Lurch. I leapt back.

Four more pairs of legs later, the scrab lay helpless on the sand, claws clacking like deadly castanets.

It was over.

We slumped against each other on the rocks, shaking and breathing hard, staring from one to another of the dying giant scrabs. Mhairie picked up another rock and smashed the heads of each of them. They twitched a few more times and then were still.

As we watched, they lost substance, in what seemed a combination of melting and evaporation, and then they were gone, leaving only the familiar scrabble of radiant green normal adults, running excitedly over the rocks.

"What just happened?" I said.

Malcolm and I both looked at Mhairie. "Ever see anything like this before?"

She shook her head. "Not myself," she said cryptically. "I've heard some stories, though."

"Did I read this wrong, or were those monsters especially angry with me?" I asked.

Neither of them spoke.

Then Malcolm said, "Did I read this wrong, or does the island wildlife want to help you out?"

"That's what's especially worrying," Mhairie said.

"Of course it is," I agreed. "Much worse than being carved up by living scissors and having your red cells exploded."

"I mean," she said, "because there's a legend."

"Of course there is," I said. Of course there was.

"But it's far too early for this to be happening again."

"What?"

"I don't even know that myself, but there's someone I know who can tell you. I'll take you tomorrow if you're fit."

And she would say no more on the subject.

They insisted on walking me home, and I did not argue. On the way we crossed Blanket Beach, where a bunch of older kids were hanging out and surfing, including Damien Duke, another California transplant (and son of my parents' biggest academic rival), who was showing off for a couple of girls that were not as pretty as Mhairie.

"Anxious Angus!" he called. "We have a wave for you. Guaranteed seaweed free!"

We ignored them. One good thing was that my new friends would probably not trash my giant roktopus story again.

My parents were both in the kitchen, which was littered with half empty packing boxes. By the looks of things, they had lost the lid of the blender, which would not blend without the lid on it. They had given up trying to find the lid, and were now focused on disabling the safety system.

"See, the lid would normally depress this lever *here*," said my dad. "So, if I use the end of this spoon to hold that down, and you switch it on…"

"*Don't!*" I yelled.

Too late. The blender whirred. Fragmented bananas, strawberries and ice cream erupted from it and painted the kitchen like a Jackson Pollock.

All five of us were gobbed with pink goo, which also ran from the walls and dripped from the ceiling.

My mom and dad began to giggle uncontrollably.

I watched with dismay as a large blob fell from the overhead light and plopped directly onto Mhairie's head, then trickled over her ringlets. This was not the kind of princess you splattered with strawberry banana shake when she came to meet your folks. Even if she had just helped you defeat a gang of overgrown, homicidal crustaceans.

Her face was haughty for a moment (which takes some doing when you have crushed fruit on your nose) but then she began to laugh as well.

It turned out to be the best thing that could have happened—three of us, weak with laughter and relief; five of us, licking and wiping up the mess. I was proud of my unusual parents, and they were happy that I had made good friends, who seemed to be normal (yeah, right), and that they had not emotionally scarred me for life by dragging me to Scotland.

I guess it was the last time I felt like a kid that summer, before I knew what was coming, and what my responsibilities would be.

Next day I would hear it from Macallister; the truth about the islands, the reason the DODO was here, the threat to reality as we knew it, and who my dad—my *original* dad—had really been.

Chapter Four

Demon Birds of Death

My sleep was dream-filled, and I woke up thinking that the scrab attack of yesterday had been one of those dreams—except that the little wounds on my chest had stuck to my pajama shirt and they nipped when I pulled it off. I threw the shirt in the washing machine so my mother wouldn't see. I didn't want to worry her. Unlike my dad and me, she was still upchucking every morning. Also she said the ground didn't feel steady under her feet, like she was on a boat or something, and couldn't stand the smell of cheese. It had been going on a bit too long to be a regular virus.

Despite the ouchy reminder on this sunny morning, yesterday's events didn't seem nearly as serious or scary as they had the day before.

Mhairie and Malcolm turned up while I was still eating my crunchies.

"I had the weirdest dream," said Malcolm. "At least, I think it was a dream. You were being eaten by a bunch of baby scrabs."

"I pulled up my sweater and showed my crusty chest."

"Jings!" he said. "That was real?"

"Just hurry up boys." Mhairie sat at the table and tapped it with her fingernails until I spooned up the last drops of sugary milk. Then she practically pushed us out of the door, almost pawing the ground with impatience.

Outside, she kept looking up at the sky, and I didn't know what she was afraid she might see there.

Little Snugglay is roughly circular, about six miles in diameter. On the South Coast there's a mountain, Ben Slumber, which has Loch Snooze at its foot. Between the Loch and The Village of Nap, where we were living, is Deep Wood, which we were advised not to explore in case we could not find our way out again and because there were still undiscovered plants and animals on the islands, some of which might be dangerous. There are beaches, some black and sparkling, some grayish white, and cliffs on the exposed West Coast; this is where the surf is rocking. The East Coast, which faces the mainland and gets less wind, has typical sand-colored sand, as well as woods and meadows.

Great Snugglay is not much larger. It has a deep West Coast bay, a craggy central hill—Ben Snore-—and a dense forest. The main DODO compound, with the central computer and a bunch of labs and offices, was on Great Snugglay. Our island, Little Snugglay, had a smaller DODO building with the dreamon drylab, where my parents worked, and the Biology Department, where Malcolm's mom did research. The two islands are separated from each other by the Slumber Strait, where the roktopi live, and each has one main village of stone cottages—Nap on the Little island and Nod on the Great one. They are each about a quarter of a mile from the Strait, well protected from winds and weather.

Mhairie's friend Macallister lived halfway up Ben Slumber. To get there, the three of us walked first along the beach where the Roktopus had spat me up, heading south towards a stretch of jagged rocks. I was still in surf jail—given my recent encounters with island wildlife, I was not too keen to get in the water anyway—but my heart sang out at the sight of the clean breakers, all the same.

"It's better than Hawaii," I said. "It's better than Indo."

"Hey baby!"

We turned. It was Damien Duke, who had appeared behind us with his board and a couple of other guys who were also big and looked dumb. Damien had to be bummed that Malcolm and I were with Mhairie, who was easily the prettiest girl on the island.

"Time to hang with cooler dudes!" he yelled, in a stunning display of originality.

It was amazing that he imagined this might work with her. She stuck her chin in the air, which she was somehow able to do without looking completely ridiculous, and kept walking.

"Wanna learn to surf?" he tried.

"Owp!" This was so off base that she let out a laugh like a bark, her seal-self giving its opinion.

"I can show you how, babe! Anxious has to stay out of the water!"

"Lay off, Duke!" I turned and faced up to him. Malcolm, who was turning out to be the kind of friend I needed, stood with me. It might have been dumb, but sometimes you have to stand up, and besides, Duke and his thugs—though they were all bigger and uglier than we were—were about twenty feet away and not coming any closer. But I figured if we showed fear, we were toast.

"Boys!" Mhairie tugged at us. "We've more important things to do!"

I knew she was right. I didn't move fast, and I didn't turn round, but I let her drag us to the jagged rocks where the thuglies could not easily follow in their bare feet. Then we turned and picked our way over the boulders, ignoring the jeers and inspired catcalls, like "Run home to Mommy, Anxious!" and "Careful you don't get your feet wet!" until they lost interest.

"Lucky for you I'm around," said Mhairie as we cleared the rocks.

"Why's that?"

"You're a dumb American rich kid"

"You got that wrong, I'm poor and smart."

"No, *I'm* poor and smart."

"What makes you so smart?"

"I wouldn't have paid for that haircut."

"It was gnawed by giant rats."

Her peal of (this time human) laughter rang out over the ocean.

"I'm not rich, either," I continued, encouraged. "My parents earn the little bucks for asking the big questions."

"Surfing *Hawaii?* Surfing *Indonesia?*"

"Those are conferences that the Grant Awards people pay for. I get to go because both of my parents are keynote speakers and they won't leave me at home. No way could we afford it otherwise."

"Och, whatever."

She batted her eyes, like—*big deal, I was still outrageously privileged.*

Once the rocks were behind us, we came to a gray-white beach that glittered with flecks of quartz, at the base of low cliffs that were also gray-white, veined in jewel colors, and pockmarked with caves.

"Ack! Ack! Ack!" A cacophony of birdcalls topped the noise of the surf.

"Those are the rokchiks," Malcolm informed me, proudly, as though he had invented them. "They live in the caves."

"Have to *go!*" insisted Mhairie

"Oh, *sweet!* No way Mhairie, you have to give me a minute," I insisted.

She sighed.

They waddled importantly on the shelves of rock and the boulders at the base of the cliffs. Hundreds of them. The adult birds were about two feet long and brilliantly colored, with fat, curved, bright blue beaks, and large, webbed, blue feet with three curved talons at the front and one at the back. Their feathers were a jumble of pink, lavender, blue and pale green—quartz colors—with some ordinary gray-white ones mixed in, especially on their fluffy chests.

Each feather was tipped with a spherical rock, the same color as the feather. They were thickly feathered, which meant they were thickly rocked—a mixture of fluff and knobble on short legs. Their blue eyes were curious and proud. They watched us, but didn't seem too worried.

Clustered around the adults' legs were white, fluffy babies, like pom-poms with beaks. Their first white rocks had just started to grow.

"They're called rokchiks because of the rocks," Malcolm said, unnecessarily. They can't fly," he went on, "because of the rocks. But if they dump the rocks, they can fly."

I had read about rokchiks, and what I didn't know Malcolm (enthusiastically) and Mhairie (reluctantly, with sighs) filled in. The rocks are made of calcium carbonate, which is formed from the combination of calcium chloride and sodium carbonate secreted from ducts in the feathers.

It's the same adaptation that's used by the roktopi, and some other island animals.

The birds live in large communities. They mate for life and lay one egg every year. They're not aggressive, unless something threatens their babies, and then they will fight to the death.

They have a strong community spirit, and will defend each other and each other's young, so they are pretty well protected and most other animals leave them alone. If they do have to fight, they can whomp hard with their rocky wings and tear with their sharp beaks and claws. As Malcolm pointed out, they usually can't fly, but if they face a fierce attacker they can release their rocks and throw them all at once—it's called a rock storm—and then they're light enough to take to the air and escape. But they will only do this when they don't have babies to guard.

I watched them for a few minutes and took pictures with Malcolm's digital. Then I figured we'd better go, before Mhairie exploded. There'd be time to come back here later.

A little ahead the beach gave way to stones again, and a rocky inlet cut between them. It was ten feet across and filled with probably twelve feet of churning water that surged when the waves rolled in.

The birds clearly thought this was great, and jostled each other to hop in and out of it. They were awesomely good swimmers and hunters, and more often than not hopped out with a big, glittering blue or green fish—of which there seemed to be an endless supply—flapping in their beaks. Standing on the rock on their short legs with their wide feet, they upended their heads and gulped the struggling fish straight down, and then waddled off to burp some of the fish back up to feed their babies.

"We have to get across that," Mhairie pointed to the rocky inlet, "which means we have to go over the cliff behind it. The climb isn't difficult, but the birds may not like us doing it too much at the moment because of the babies. Watch your step, don't make sudden moves, and *don't step on a baby!*"

Malcolm and I looked at each other, uneasily. "OK," we said.

Fortunately, there were not many babies close to the inlet. They mostly hung back, where it was safe and dry, waiting for regurgitated yummies. We clambered carefully, Mhairie in front, me in the middle, and Malcolm behind, to where the inlet dead-ended and we could get over the rocks to the next part of the beach.

"Ack! Ack! Ack!" said the rokchiks. They weren't rattled at all, but chattered quietly and flat-footed around us. It was neat to be this close. A couple of them nuzzled the legs of my jeans with their razor sharp beaks, and one dropped a fat purple fish at my feet. Too late, I stepped on it and slid down hard on my fanny. Malcolm grabbed me, or I would have slipped into the frothing water, and my weight pulled him down as well. He hit badly on his right knee. "Ahh!"

Mhairie turned back and braced against a rock to help us without going down herself.

"Ackle! Ackle! Ackle! Ackle! Ackle!" the birds clucked, wildly agitated.

My palms were skinned and my heart was thumping. Malcolm sat, his back against a boulder, still holding on to me. The knee of his jeans was torn and the scrape inside must have hurt like heck, even worse with the salt water in it. His face was gray with pain.

There was a stretch in front of us that was slick with seaweed, and sloped down into the frothing trench. We stayed put for a minute, breathing heavily, assessing the situation. The obvious thing to do was to climb up away from the seaweed, and go over a higher part of the cliff where it was dry, but it wasn't clear how much Malcolm's knee could handle. My sore hands wouldn't help much, either.

The tide was coming in and our path back was cut off already. Soon our perch was going to be under water. We had to go forward, and quickly.

"Ackle! Ackle! Ackle," said the rokchiks to each other, and a couple of them flapped their wings. They gathered in front of us, in a concerned huddle.

Then the big one that had dropped the purple fish waddled out onto the seaweed stretch, and started shaking and hopping from one foot to the other in a funny little dance. Its rocks began dropping off. They scattered on the seaweed and stuck there. Then the bird, newly rockless, flapped in earnest and took flight, circling us a couple of times before swooping down to stand on a boulder, acking excitedly.

A bunch of feathers slowly settled onto the rock-strewn seaweed stretch.

"Ack! Ack! Ack! Ack! Ack!" squawked the other birds. One by one, they repeated the performance, scattering rocks and feathers across the seaweed, then soaring into the air, clearly thrilled by the unaccustomed lightness.

Soon the seaweed-covered rock was completely buried in a layer of brightly colored, calcium carbonate pebbles, mixed up with pastel fluff. It looked like a kid's art box. The birds started stepping across it, looking back at us to show us what to do. The chunks didn't roll or slide under the birds' weight. They were stuck to the seaweed.

"Jings!" said Mhairie. It was pretty unusual for her to be surprised by anything.

Fish Dropper continued to walk back and forth, across the path they had made for us, while the other birds flapped up and down, guarding the edge, clearly ready to push back if one of us did slip. A few of them flew behind us, and gently nudged us on.

"Do you think you can do it Malcolm?" I said.

Gingerly, he flexed his knee. "Not broken, no torn ligaments. I can go."

We went across on all fours—me using my hands as little as possible, Malcolm keeping his right knee off the ground, the rokchiks flapping beside us ackling kindly.

We made it to the other side. The rokchiks were very proud, strutting around with their rockless chests puffed out, swooping and soaring victoriously.

"Thanks, guys," I stood up and spoke to them. "Thank you. From the heart." I put my hands over my heart, which was a bit lame, but it seemed to please them. They ackled and nodded, did a few more farewell swoops, then flapped off back to their fish and their babies, and to grow themselves more rocks.

Ahead of us was soft, white sand. Malcolm stood up and tested his weight on his knee. "The worst of it's over," he said. "The shock's wearing off; I can walk. Won't be running any marathons this week, though."

"Certainly are a hit around here, Anxious Angus," Mhairie remarked, but she didn't sound pleased. For some reason, it worried her that the birds had wanted to help us—that they had wanted to help *me*.

We headed inland towards Ben Slumber, Malcolm limping a bit but not complaining, and Mhairie making the effort to control her impatience.

I had been feeling happy and free, but now something was eating at me—like I was worried there was something I should be worried about. My mind kept trying to grab it, but missed. I started to remember all the other things that were strange about the islands that I had been ignoring.

"Did you feel sick when you first came here, Malcolm?"

"My whole family had the flu for a week."

He was looking more serious as well, maybe because of his knee.

"Us, too."

We both looked at Mhairie. She shrugged. "Don't look at me, I'm a Selkie. I never gave you the flu."

"And what about the dreams? We've all been having strange ones—not nightmares—dreams that feel like they really happened."

"Right," said Malcolm. "My mum dreamt she had a patient with a disease that she's an expert in, and she mooned about the infirmary for days looking for that patient, but he didn't exist. She still remembers him and his X-rays."

"And then sometimes you think you've dreamed something that really did happen. Like the scrab attack."

"Exactly!" said Malcolm.

Mhairie sighed and said under her breath, "Saps are so difficult to work with."

"*What* did you call us?"

"Saps. As in *Homo sapiens*? Which I'm not one of, no offence intended."

There was no answer to that, so instead I said, "What's your Latin name then?"

"I don't have a Latin name."

"Every species has a Latin name," Malcolm insisted.

"I'm not a species. I'm a myth or legend." She shook her black curls.

After a minute, Malcolm said, "Sorry, my myth take."

She gave him a look that said *Earthworm* and I thought for sure she'd be in the huff for an hour at least, but then her mouth quivered and her peal of silvery laughter rang out.

I poked Malcolm in the ribs to say *Good one!* He was flushed with success.

"Are you really from Benbecula, Mhairie?" I took advantage of her good mood to fish for information.

"I said I was."

"But are you really?" I pressed. "Because this story about people from other islands moving in to an uninhabited village that was just conveniently here and in perfect condition when the DODO arrived is hard to swallow."

She shrugged again. "Selkies like our privacy."

"Right," I said. "Privacy."

But it seemed to me that people—Selkies, whatever—had always been here but they just didn't want to answer awkward questions.

Then there was the issue of the maps. The Snugglays were clearly marked on new ones and you could look them up on the Internet, but they did not appear on maps that were more than six months old. They were talked about in some old Scottish Legends, but not in travel books or academic texts. A bunch of people had noticed this of course, and the story was that the islands had somehow been overlooked by traditional mapmaking techniques. They had been detected because of strong signals recorded by computer equipment—partly designed by my parents—that was programmed to detect dreamon energy. Clear, though undecipherable sequences of code had registered on computers in diverse locations and ultimately led to the mapping of the Snugglays.

"It sounds a bit hokey," Malcolm agreed. "When you put it like that."

"You think? Mhairie, what's going on here?"

"And what happened twelve years ago?" Malcolm said suddenly, as though he had just snapped awake.

"Twelve years ago?"

"I heard it from some of the other kids," he explained. "Some story about a terrible land and sea battle here in the Hebrides, with monsters like—well, like your roktopus." He winced apologetically. "I just assumed it was a story, or exaggeration at best."

There were also the older legends: the Snugglay Islands, Isles of Dreams, shadowy landmasses that rose in the Atlantic once every century or so, bringing fear, confusion, and terrible beasties, and the threat of war from a Dark Lord. The Scottish Government said they had named the newly discovered Snugglays after these legendary islands. Bad mistake, in my humble opinion.

"So how about it, Mhairie? What's the deal on this? Spill."

"Angus," she said finally, and it might have been the first time she had used my real name, "I can't explain these things to you. I'm not old enough to remember them. Macallister will tell you everything."

And I had to accept that, for the time being—which wasn't difficult, given what was just about to take my attention.

Loch Snooze is a splash of sparkling silver at the foot of Ben Slumber, which rolls greenly up to a soft, majestic height. On this day the green was patched with pink and purple heather, and smoke curled from the chimney of a stone cottage about halfway up the slope.

"Macallister lives up there," whispered Mhairie.

"Why are we whispering?" I whispered back.

"The potami are sleeping, which suits me just fine. We don't need the distraction. Now, come on."

"Oh, come on yourself," said Malcolm. "He needs to see the potami."

"What potami?"

"*Sleepy*potami. Och! You woke them up!"

Some of the patches of pink and purple heather stood up and stretched, then dropped to all fours.

"Whoa!" I said.

Malcolm grinned, and took my picture. Mhairie sighed.

The sleepypotami, stretched out flat, had the dimensions of an average throw rug. In the up position, they were the size of a

St. Bernard, but with shorter, shaggy legs, fluffy bodies, big feet that ended in five golden, retractable claws, and little swingy tails. They had flat, shaggy heads with little ears, soft noses, and bright blue eyes that sparkled with intelligence. Their faces were sort of like koalas.

They shook themselves, like pink and purple waterfalls, and immediately began to plod excitedly up the hill. When they got to a height that was comfortable for them, they curled up into shaggy pastel balls and rolled down again, gathering speed on the grassy slope all the way to the overhang that jutted over the loch like a natural diving board. They bounced off it, seeming to rise a little in the air before they splashed into Snooze, and disappeared below the surface for a moment before bouncing out in spread-eagle form and flopping back to float and paddle for a few minutes. Then they clambered out onto the shingle, shook the water off and diligently rolled themselves completely dry on the grass before plodding up the hill to repeat the process and get themselves wet all over again.

"Wheee!" they cried on the way down the hill. "Whaa! Whoo!"

On the lower slopes many of the creatures were clearly babies, the littlest ones snuggled up to a protective parent. The parents patted the babies showing them how to tuck in their feet and heads, then gave them a little push and ran to the overhang, watching anxiously until the little ones popped up, squeaking with pleasure.

The commotion at the bottom of the hill woke up more and more of the potami that were sleeping higher up. When these potami rolled, they reached breathtaking speeds and shot off the overhang flying tens of feet over the loch before they splashed down.

Amazingly, there were almost no collisions except for little bumps between the learning infants. It was as if they had a spatial sense, which allowed them to steer around each other even when balled up and cannoning down a mountainside. And I guess they did.

I watched, captivated and completely forgetting my worries of a few minutes ago, while Malcolm kept up the running commentary: "The wee ones are the babies. The mothers are teaching the babies. When the ones at the bottom shout, it wakes up the ones higher up. They like to get dry before they do it again."

Mhairie's shoulders slumped and she sat on a rock, from time to time looking at her watch. But she had calmed down a good bit now that Macallister's house was actually in sight, and when Malcolm said, "Brilliant! They've noticed us!" the big sigh that she gave was more like something she felt she had to do, to keep up appearances.

One wet, happy baby bounded over like a puppy. She (she was female, according to Mhairie) leapt at me, I caught her and she started to dry herself on my shirt. I laughed, trying to hold on to her while keeping my face away from the soggy fur.

More babies flopped over to us, moving like big rabbits, and started drying themselves on our jeans. Then a couple of the adults lumbered over and nuzzled our hands. The babies squeaked and pulled at Mhairie—it was clear that she was a friend of theirs—and she broke down and started to actually smile. She looked up at the cottage, where a figure stood in the open doorway, and the last of the tension went out of her shoulders.

"Oh, all right," she said. She kicked her shoes off and slipped gracefully behind a rock, then reappeared almost immediately, this time awkwardly on her flippers and tail. I still have no idea how she does this, or where her clothes go when she turns into a seal. This is not the kind of princess that you ask, etc....

"Owp!" she barked triumphantly, and flopped into the loch flipping a spray of droplets at us with her tail.

She cut under the water like a torpedo, then surfaced directly under a big, basking potamus that rose in the air with delighted squawks, then balled itself up as it hit the water, bobbing. Mhairie began pushing it around with her nose. The other potami rolled up too, and clamored for attention. Clearly, they were used to this game.

I would have liked to join in, but Malcolm's knee was obviously hurting him, and I was still a bit uneasy about getting into the water—although at this point I couldn't quite remember why. So we stood on the pebbly shore and watched the pink and purple furry football game for five minutes or so.

And then the weather changed.

Something sucked the brightness out of the day and a low, howling wind began to circle.

All of the potamis' ears flipped up at the same time.

Mhairie was out of the water and behind her rock, zipping out of her seal-self in one fluid movement. She kicked the skin onto Loch Snooze, where it floated for a moment, then slowly sank.

"Up the hill!" she scolded us, pushing her feet into her shoes, furious with herself for having had fun.

She didn't need to tell us twice. We started climbing. I heard Malcolm grunt, and hung back with him.

"No, go!" he said. "I'll catch you up!"

"Angus, he's right!" said Mhairie. "It's you that needs to get to Macallister!"

The potami all clambered out of the water and flip-flopped up the hill, pushing us with encouraging, concerned, *whaas* and *whoos*.

They seemed to emerge from the mountain itself— two enormous rokchiks, blocking our path to Macallister's cottage. They were fifteen feet tall, purple, green and gold, with beaks like scythes and talons like meat hooks. The stems of their feathers were flexible and strong, like some kind of industrial plastic, and the rocks attached to them were the size of baseballs; hard, shiny and multifaceted, like brilliant chunks of sharp-edged, colored glass.

Their black eyes glittered like vicious chips of onyx. All four of them glittered at me.

Memories slammed into me—the roktopus, the scrabs— as the monstrous avians began to walk towards me, hen-toed on their giant, wicked feet, deadly beaks preparing to slash and tear.

Everything that happened next happened in just a few seconds.

Six or seven sleepypotami jumped the nearest terror bird— one on its back, one on its tail, a couple on each wing. A big, muscular purple potami shrieked a battle cry—"Whaaa!" and threw itself at the rokchik's chest, hugging it fiercely. The bird snatched the potamus with its curving beak, pulled him off its body, and flung him away—the potamus clutching rocks and feathers in his four clawed feet as he flew. He hit an exposed boulder and slid flat on the grass, not moving.

Next, the bird flapped its great wings and the potami clinging to them were thrown off to land in the grass, stunned but with pawfuls of brilliant gems. More potami leapt on the monster, and were thrown off in the same way. The rocks and feathers regrew almost immediately. The potami were keeping the bird busy, but they were not wearing it out.

In the meantime, the little sleepypotamus that had been so friendly sprang up and clung to my neck, and Mhairie and Malcolm stepped between the second giant bird and me.

"Stay away from him, you overgrown chicken!" Mhairie yelled.

"No!" I shouted, trying to pull the little potamus off me gently.

"Get behind it!" Mhairie said. "Stay away from the beak and the wings. It needs the tail for balance. Get the tail! Don't grab the rocks!"

She and Malcolm circled behind it and grabbed its long tail feathers, close to the skin. The bird couldn't reach them with its beak.

"Ack! Ack! Ack!" the rokchik shrieked, flapping. It swung its tail, trying to shake them off, but they held fast.

But it didn't make any difference, except to make the monster even madder. It focused on me again and advanced, not even slowed down, dragging my friends behind it.

Then it lifted its wings and clapped them. A storm of deadly jewels lit the air as they rocketed at me. I turned and ducked my head, bracing, and folding my body around the little animal that wanted to protect me.

A split second later, the projectiles hit. The impacts were sharp as the edges cut skin, and dull as my bones absorbed the shocks. They struck my back, my legs, my bare arms, and the back of my neck. One of them caught my left ear. I reeled and went down on my knees. Another hit my head; warm blood ran down over my vertebrae, under my shirt.

Malcolm let go of the tail and ran to help me. I didn't see what happened next. So you'll have to take Malcolm's word for it.

A dark figure ran from the cottage, and scrambled down the hill. He held a small, black object in his right hand, He ran past the rokchik that was still throwing potami, past the rokchik that was dragging Mhairie and Malcolm, and reached me just as it raised its wings to hurl a second volley of freshly grown crystals. He dropped to his knees in front of me, put his hand on my head and extended the dark cylinder.

A disturbance, which Malcolm described as "a pulse of wavy air," slid out from the weapon and met the bird's chest.

The gray feathers there ruffled outwards, in concentric circles like a cornfield hit by a meteor.

The bird looked down at itself, over its beak, and squawked a furious "Ack! Ack! Ack!"

And then it began to dissolve: from the point of contact outward, it melted into the air. Malcolm could see through the hole that grew in its body to Mhairie's astonished face behind it, and then more and more of the hillside, grass and daisies, and less and less of the rokchik until it completely disappeared.

Macallister pointed the beam at the other giant bird, which was now completely covered in a furry pile of angry sleepypotami.

"Don't hurt them!" screamed Mhairie.

But the pulse passed harmlessly through the potami. It got the rokchik underneath them, though. Malcolm couldn't see it, but apparently it vanished like the first one, because suddenly the potami were smothering nothing, and fell on top of each other in a pink and purple heap.

It was over. The day was bright and gentle again. The potami picked themselves up and shook their fur, nuzzling each other.

"Don't move, son," Macallister warned, as I came to and tried to stand up. The little sleepypotamus whimpered and rubbed her soft nose on my face.

Mhairie and Malcolm checked me over, anxiously. "He's OK, I think," Malcolm said.

"I feel like a tenderized steak," I said, weakly. Lame joke, but it was important to make the effort. I got slowly to my feet. "Thanks by the way," I told Macallister.

"Any time," he replied. "And by the way, I'm a vegetarian."

We all laughed, more from relief than the inspired wit.

But a few feet away, things were not going so well. Several

of the potami had been injured, and were limping and wheeping, but they'd recover—except for one. The big, brave purple guy who'd been first to jump on the monster had not moved since his head hit that boulder—and he was never going to move again.

The others crowded round him, pawing him gently, making anguished howls and yips. The little one who had stayed with me flopped over to the group, sniffing and nuzzling the dead hero, crying quietly.

Mhairie, Malcolm and I stood with Macallister, quietly shocked, taking it in.

It was the first actual death of the summer. It brought home to all of us that there was mortal danger here.

"Can we help them?" I asked Macallister.

"We should leave them alone now," he said. "Respect their grief. They have their own response to death, and it's private.

"In the meantime, son, we'd better get you inside. You have a lot to learn, and I have a short time to teach you."

The gravity in his weathered face chilled me almost more than the dead sleepypotamus. We helped each other to the cottage, where I would get my questions answered, and learn my enemy's name.

Chapter Five

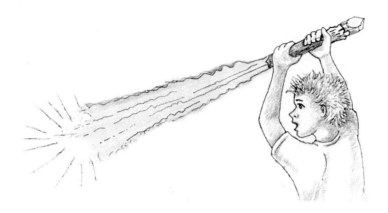

Freako Creatures Eat The Beach

"I should have brought them straight up the hill," said Mhairie, as soon as we got inside.

"No, it's my fault Mhairie," Macallister said in his mellow Scottish voice. "I thought they wouldn't attack again so quickly."

"What?" Malcolm and I demanded together.

Macallister's face was heavily lined, but from other things like his movements, his voice and his body, I put him at about the same age as my dad. His black hair was unruly and graying at the sides. He was thin, and wore a rumpled gray sweater with the sleeves pushed up.

The room we were in had old, comfortable furniture and objects from different parts of the world like Chinese wall hangings and bright, carved animals from India. The beat-up sofa was covered with a red and blue Mexican rug; the walls were lined with shelves made of planks balanced on bricks that held what must have been thousands of books. They were on every subject you could think of, but the biggest sections were poetry, biology and physics.

At the back of the room were a table with a loaf of bread, a hunk of cheese, and a pitcher with blue stars at one end and a microscope at the other. Behind the table, one wall was lined with advanced looking computer equipment.

"Let's get you cleaned up and I'll explain everything," he said.

The cuts on the back of my head and my ear had stopped bleeding. There were some little cuts on my arms that Macallister put band-aids on. He gave me a clean blue shirt and I washed and changed in the bathroom, which had white tiles and a claw-footed tub. I looked at myself in the scratched mirror. There were yellow bruises and scrapes left over from the roktopus, purple scrapes and scabs from yesterday's encounter with the scrabs, and the fresh injuries from today. I walked back into the living room.

"For a start," I said to Macallister, "where can I get one of *those?*" I pointed to the black cylinder that he had dissolved the rokchiks with.

Macallister looked up from bandaging Malcolm's knee. Malcolm had cut the legs off his jeans rather than take them off in front of Mhairie (though I doubt that she cared one way or the other, and was absorbed in a book called, *Hunting Techniques of the Orca*) so he was now wearing shorts.

"Good as new," he said, testing the knee with his weight.

Macallister put the object in my hand. "This one's yours. It's no use to me."

"You just used it to kill two demon birds of doom."

"Because I was touching you," he said. "The Blackflash won't work for anyone else. Your dad left it for you."

Things were coming together rapidly. "What happened twelve years ago?"

"Sit down Angus," he said gently. "This won't be easy to hear."

He unlocked a drawer in a red lacquered cabinet with dragon carvings on it and took out a thick, worn black book, which he put in my hands.

I looked at the cover for a minute, then got my act together and opened it. Inside was a picture of a pretty dark haired girl—Arla MacDream, my original mom. *Diary of Hamish MacDream* was written on the flyleaf.

"Your father was my best friend," Macallister said.

After a minute I said, "So how did he die?"

"He was killed on this island twelve years ago, fighting the denizens of Dwam."

"Denizens of Dwam?"

"Monsters like the rokchiks that attacked you today. When I took his body back to the mainland your biological mother went into labor early. She had time enough to pour all the love she had into you, and then she died as well."

"Tell me how he died." I said.

"How much do you know about what your adoptive parents and the DODO are doing here?"

I explained about the dreamons, going into a bit more detail than I had for Mhairie and Malcolm before. Basically my "new" parents believed that these dreamons were particle-wave-particles, which among other things, affect the human brain. Their starting point for this hypothesis was the difference between memories and dreams; most dreams being difficult to remember, even when you wake up with them fresh in your mind, and when you do remember them they have an unreal quality.

"Except here," said Malcolm.

"Except here," I agreed.

My parents reasoned that these dreams must have a different physical basis than memories, and were probably the result

of an outside influence. Their theory was that the dreamons
drifted around in clouds, passing through peoples' skulls and
influencing their thought patterns, especially while they were
asleep. They also postulated that under certain circumstances,
the dreamons could be organized into something like a
computer file that once inside your head, could play like a
movie. So they figured that a computer with the right program
should be able to pick up these files and translate them. If this
turned out to be true, it should be possible for computers to
broadcast dreams into peoples' heads.

"You can see why the American military might find that
interesting," Mhairie said drily.

"I guess," I shrugged.

"Not bad," Macallister said. "They've got it partly right."

The other part, Macallister explained, was that the
dreamons could be organized into creatures with physical
mass. Mostly, the dreamon clouds (which Macallister called
Dwam substance) swirled around aimlessly, but the particle-
wave-particles were sticky; every so often a bunch of them
would click together in an unexpected way—like the
difference between a pile of bricks and a house—and slowly
an organic structure would grow. An "organizing intelligence"
always emerged, and these were always remarkably similar
to each other. The Selkies called them "Murky Harry." In
normal circumstances it took about one hundred years for
a Harry to develop. Harry could shape the dreamons into
creatures—denizens of Dwam—that he used to promote his
world takeover plan.

My real dad and Macallister had been at University together
in Glasgow when some hokey stories hit the press. A couple of
fishing boats had been destroyed in bad weather; the survivors
came back with tales of giant, knobbly octopi and islands that
were not on a map.

At University, my real dad was doing his PhD on Scottish myths and legends with a section devoted to the then still mythical Snugglays. As the legend tells it, every hundred years or so from when recorded history began, there were stories of islands appearing where there had been none before, boats being wrecked, and megabeasts attacking the other islands and sometimes the mainland as well. The beasts always had a leader who appeared to be human who was called "Murky Harry" by the locals. There was also always a hero, who rose to defeat him in a hand-to-hand fight to the death.

My real dad persuaded Macallister to check it out with him. As well as being great material for his thesis, it was going to be his last adventure before he had a wean to cramp his style. (Wean is Scottish for baby, by which he meant me).

The two men from Barra who piloted them to Little Snugglay in a motor launch were very grave and said they were doing it because somebody had to stand up. But they didn't make it—a sea snake the size of a tram broke the boat in half and that was the end of them. The Selkies rescued my dad and Macallister.

"So the Snugglays *were* inhabited then!" I said, looking at Mhairie, who was listening very carefully.

"The Selkies have always been here," Macallister said. "They keep watch."

"But why the secrecy? Why pretend they're from somewhere else?"

Macallister and Mhairie both looked at me, like, *Duh!*

"Because they're Selkies," said Macallister.

"If the Saps knew we were here the place would be an amusement park," said Mhairie. "Or maybe we'd be in the zoo."

They had fake addresses on the other islands, so they could telecommute and do Open University courses. I had to admit it made sense.

Macallister continued telling the story:

The Selkies had been expecting my dad, and recognized him for who he was. When the sea snake that had killed the two Barra men slithered out of the water and over the beach, whipping its muscular tail and stabbing with its long fangs, the Selkies told him, "Only you can kill it—with this!" and pressed a piece of green island quartz into his hand.

At first, nothing happened, but as the snake advanced the quartz began to glow, and had a halo of distorted air around it.

The snake seemed to know who my dad was as well, and was making straight for him. Macallister yelled and threw rocks, but they bounced harmlessly off its hide.

With a sudden sense of knowingness, my dad waited until the giant snake was almost on him, then lunged for it, pressing the quartz into its head between the eyes. The monster stopped dead, shivered, and began to blur, dissolving in sections from the head back until only the tail was left to disappear with a slight pop.

For a few days after that, my dad and Macallister learned all they could from the Selkies. None of them had been alive during the last invasion, but the Selkies all knew about the denizens of Dwam, Murky Harry, and how only one hero could kill Harry with the island quartz. They had been preparing for the battle to happen in their lifetimes.

Macallister made a big contribution when he built the Blackflash, which amplified the quartz's power and could focus it into a beam. Almost intuitively, my dad learned how to use it from a distance or like a sword if he wanted.

During the siege of the Dwam there was an attack from some new freako creature about once a day—a six-foot scorpohamster with an eight-foot stinger, a swarm of biting rokroaches the size of cats, and a Caledonian MacBrayne Ferry was sunk by two giant roktopi, forcing my dad and Macallister to take a boat out and fight them at sea. The attacks were not prolonged, and the Selkies said their purpose was to wear my dad out and soften him up before the big one.

Then there was quiet for a few days, which the Selkies said meant the denizens were gathering strength.

When they came in full force it was on a night that was cold and still. Blood chilling acking shattered the silence. Selkies spilled out of their cottages and down to Blanket Beach ready to fight, where a dozen terror birds waited in a line at the base of the cliffs, their jagged rocks glinting in the moonlight and their beaks jabbing viciously as they hen-toed forwards, while waves of giant scrabs rushed from the rocks that bounded each side of the bay, and at the same time monster roktopi rose from the ocean cutting off all routes of escape.

Because of Macallister's great military instinct and awesome brain, he had downloaded every piece of information the Selkies had that could be useful. They knew that as Murky Harry gained strength, the denizens would start to become creatures of this world, making it harder to destroy them with energy using the Blackflash, but at the same time more vulnerable to mortal injury. This meant that Macallister and the Selkies would be able to fight alongside my dad.

Denizens that were dissipated by the Blackflash or killed in mortal combat would completely disappear, but more would keep taking their place unless Harry was defeated. Meantime, those that were only injured would continue to exist; though useless to fight, they continued to sap Harry's energy.

Key to Murky Harry's tactics was to wear the defenders out with onslaught after onslaught of denizens until they were completely exhausted, then to deliver the deathblow to the hero and complete the invasion.

Key to Macallister's defense was to disable, but not kill the denizens, draining Harry's resources and forcing him to fight my dad earlier than he wanted to.

Macallister recounted the battle:

Selkies in human form held off the scrabs that were coming from the north and south with thrown rocks or in hand-to-hand combat. Most of them had brought useful weapons: kitchen scissors and shears that they used to cut the eyestalks and the spindly legs. Cutting or tearing the eyes off was the most effective way of dealing with them: the arthropods then skittered around, shrieking and slashing at whatever was in reach, usually the leg or stinger of another scrab. These scrabs were hurt but not dead, so they didn't disappear. The Selkies piled them up in hills of struggling, snapping bodies that the fresh monsters had to climb over to get to the beach, putting themselves at risk of breakage by thrown rocks.

Meantime, the Selkies in seal form tackled the roktopi that were still in the ocean. Selkies are immune to roktopus toxin, and can swim very fast. They darted around the agitated tentacles, infuriating the molluscs, which began to shoot their rocks violently into the water so that the sea was filled with hurtling green and purple projectiles. The Selkies surfaced and made for shore, riding the waves above the rock storm, while the roktopi were caught in it. Whump! Whump! The huge, sensitive eyes were bruised and smashed by flying gems, and soon the would-be invaders were a blinded, viciously thrashing tangle of knobbly bodies and rubbery, living whips.

The Sea Dwammers that had already made it to the beach were harder to deal with. Roktopi the size of garbage trucks scuttled horribly on their tentacles, grabbing Selkies in seal or human form, dashing them cruelly on the rocks. My dad took care of them, cutting them down with the beam of the Blackflash. Their bodies did not disappear immediately, but lay jerking and hissing on the grit for a few minutes before dissolving into the air.

Then my dad turned to face the line of rokchiks advancing from the cliffs. This was the biggest challenge for the defending army, as Macallister had known it would be.

My dad dissipated the first and then the second rokchik with the Blackflash beam, the way Macallister had done when he saved us on Ben Slumber. Immediately another two emerged from the cliff to take their place. There were too many of them for my dad to hold off by himself. They were attacking the Selkies, throwing their rocks from a distance, wounding them, then swooping down to finish them off with their talons and beaks.

Macallister had theorized a plan—it was untested and there was no knowing if it would work, but it was worth a try. In their rush to the beach a group of Selkies had carried every fire extinguisher from the village. Praying that it would work, Macallister gave the order for them to shoot the stone-feathered horrors with the soft white foam.

It worked amazingly well! The birds—covered in the fluffy substance that also filled their open beaks—stumbled around, shaking their heads, spitting and gurgling furiously like gigantic, animated soap-bubble sculptures.

Even more excellent, the chemicals in the extinguisher foam reacted somehow with their liquid rock-producing ducts, and stuck their rocks and feathers together so that they couldn't chuck their rocks or even flap their wings.

The Selkies cheered. Then a new line of rokchiks appeared, angrier and more wicked looking than the first. If they kept it up, eventually the Resistance would run out of foam and become birdseed.

But then Murky Harry appeared.

He was dark, thin, black-caped and hook-nosed. He emerged from the shadows as though he was made of them—which I guess he was. His breath was a hiss that could be heard over the sound of the sea. He was barely in control of his rage, and trembled with it, surrounded by his disabled terror force that was struggling and sapping his strength.

My dad raised his Blackflash and its pulse of wavy air extended into a blade about three feet long. Harry's lips twisted into something between a sneer and a snarl. He made a claw of his hand, which filled up with darkness that he threw at my dad. The darkball whizzed at him, blacker than night, trailing smoke and ragged edges. My dad's blade hit and sliced it in two. It fizzed and vanished in a blur of ash and an acrid electrical smell filled the air.

At the same time the beam of the Blackflash cracked like lightning, then cut out. My dad rocked backwards, absorbing the shock. Then he squared his shoulders and the beam slid out of the Blackflash again.

Harry threw another and another. My dad slashed and the Blackflash beam shorted out again as it hit and destroyed one darkball. My dad went down on one knee, and Harry's next shot went over his head and splashed on a boulder in runny, black slime. The boulder began to fizzle and dissolve in puffs of evil smelling smoke. My dad looked back at it quickly in shock, then braced for the next volley.

It went like that for minutes that must have seemed like hours—Harry hurling, my dad slicing and dodging. They were evenly matched and they were both slowing up.

No new Dwam denizens formed; the old ones were getting blurry at the edges. The Selkies and Macallister were winning that fight.

Meantime, Harry was throwing darkballs slower and slower, and my dad was close to exhaustion; the Blackflash beam was only a few inches long. Then Harry made a fatal mistake. Realizing that his army was almost spent, knowing that if he lost here it would take a century before he built up enough strength to break into reality again, he raised both hands above his head, allowing them to fill with an enormous collection of dark that he clearly meant to overwhelm my dad and the Blackflash with in an all-or-nothing assault.

My dad took the all-or-nothing approach as well. Summoning the last of his strength he allowed the Blackflash to die back, then forced a long beam out of it, pushing it at Harry's chest. It caught him just under the ribcage. The huge gob of darkslime dropped from Harry's raised hands and slid over his own head and shoulders. As he looked down at himself, his mouth a horrified O, he began to dissolve from the inside out.

It was over. The Dwam denizens spitting and hissing on the destroyed beach gradually evaporated. Many Selkies were dead or badly hurt, but they had defended their homeland against the invasion of Dwam and protected their children's future.

"Then Murky Harry didn't kill my father!" I shouted. "So, how did he die?"

"It happened a few days later," Macallister explained. "Not all of the denizens left when Harry died."

At least two Dwam denizens had a strong enough presence in reality to survive Harry's dissipation for several more days. One was a smallish giant roktopus that showed up when some Selkie mothers were down on Bolster Bay teaching their babies to swim.

My dad and Macallister were there too, practicing improvements to the Blackflash and generally resting up until a boat was made ready to take them back to the mainland.

The roktopus emerged from the waves, confused without its leader and enraged by the activity at the shoreline. It grabbed a white, fluffy baby with one tentacle and began to flap her around in the air.

The Selkie mother owped in panic and threw herself at the beast, which batted her fifteen feet away into the ocean.

My dad aimed the Blackflash at the body mass, between the eyes. The mollusk quivered, and a small hole appeared in its head and began to grow, but this denizen had a strong connection to the physical world and would take longer to disrupt. It continued to hold the terrified baby out of reach while thwacking its tentacles at the other distressed seal folk.

My dad heard the harsh "Cacaw, Cacaw!" before he saw the second of the remaining denizens. A reagle, with a twenty-foot wingspan, sharp-pointed feathers, and talons like knives, swooped down from nowhere, clutched his shoulders and lifted him off the ground. Too late, Macallister grabbed for his friend. My dad could have saved himself then, but he chose the baby Selkie and kept the Blackflash beam trained on the roktopus. The hole in its head expanded until its borders vanished and the baby splashed, unhurt, into the water and her mother's tearful embrace. By this time the reagle had flown my dad too high off the ground for the fall to be survivable. It soared off with him, cacawing triumphantly over the cliffs.

Macallister hoped the beast would land somewhere and my dad would get the chance to fight it.

"How did he die?" I asked, quietly.

"It dropped him," said Macallister. "He was dropped."

And that was that. No last words. No final message for his son. The diary was all I was going to get, and I had to accept it.

Everybody was quiet for a few minutes. I avoided the sympathy in Mhairie's big eyes.

Malcolm broke the silence. "So this Dwam. It's like an alternative reality?"

"No, that's not right," Macallister said. "There may be alternative realities, but if so, they are complete realities. Why would they want to break into this one? It's not that great. Dwam exists *outside* reality. When Harry and the denizens form, their only way to continue existing is to take over our world."

I had to admit, that was strong motivation.

"And why here?" Malcolm insisted. "Why the Snugglays?"

"That I can't answer," Macallister said. "Either the energy's especially strong here, or the skin on reality's weak."

Macallister had completed his PhD on the physics of the Aurora Borealis—that's the Northern Lights to you and me—then returned to the island to continue his private research on the nature of Dwam. He hadn't expected to be alive for the next invasion, and was planning to leave a store of information with the Selkies and some cool new hardware for the next hero.

"But," he said grimly, "whatever your people are doing, it's speeded things up."

He taught me how to use the Blackflash, which had the size, weight and appearance of a rubberized pocket flashlight.

"The island quartz," he explained, "has a molecular structure that amplifies a particle-wave-particle pattern from your brain that can disrupt denizens. It's a bit like a computer file and only your brain produces it. I'm betting that if we went back through history, we'd find that you're directly related to every Snugglay hero. Switch it on."

There was no switch.

"You have to think."

"I *am* thinking."

"You have to *push* it with your mind."

Oh boy. Particle-wave-particles. Dreamons. I was out of patience with this stuff. Why couldn't it be a regular laser with a switch to turn it on and a switch to turn it off? Or an infrared death ray. Something simple.

But then I felt heat from the thing in my hand, and a slight vibration. Against my better judgment, my mind was pushing. Or maybe it was just being pulled.

A waviness beamed out of the object like a distortion of the air. It looked something like a heat haze, but focused in a thin, flat line about two inches wide and three feet long, that tapered to a point. You could only call it a blade.

"Now, the deal is this—" Macallister said, "when Dwam is young, only you can kill the denizens. As they mature, they can be attacked by physical means as well—most of them are at that stage right now, probably because the DODO activities have sped things up. This means the battle for reality will happen soon. Harry can't sustain them at this level for very long, so he'll have to make his move. If they cross over completely, the Blackflash won't work at all. But if that happens, we'll have bigger problems. Anyone left alive will be a visitor in Dwam."

"Right," I acknowledged. "That wouldn't be good."

After that we sat around for a while and talked to Macallister. None of us wanted to leave his company. Even without his importance to the survival of life as we knew it, I'd have wanted to know him and I could see that Malcolm was stoked. They had a couple of conversations that were way over my head.

Macallister did answer some of my burning questions. For example, it was true that people here got dreams and reality mixed up, and when they saw a Dwam denizen they usually thought it was a dream and forgot about it the next day. This had happened to my dad and him as well, until after the second or third life-threatening encounter. After that, things changed and they remembered everything. Macallister figured that Malcolm and I were probably at that point already.

"And Mhairie," he added, "being not actually human—or maybe she is human, but something else as well—is unaffected."

"Can Dwam make people actually sick?" I suddenly asked. I was thinking about my mom. Macallister didn't know, but looked very serious when I told him about the forgetfulness, the throwing up, the cold sweats, and the weird feelings. If she didn't get better, he said, we should find a way to get her off the island.

When he was not pursuing his physics, Macallister studied some of the island's exotic creatures. Now, this is what floats my boat and it was clearly as interesting to Malcolm as the nature of Dwam. It occurred to me that Malcolm was very much like Macallister and I realized with a small shock how lucky I was to have him for a friend.

On the floor next to the microscope was a large tank filled with ratty mangroid leaves that were pockmarked with holes and gobs of slime. Six or seven spiky green caterpillars—about the size of my finger—inched around on them, chewing efficiently. As we watched, one shot a dollop of black from its tail end that flew several inches to strike another part of the leaf. The plant substance instantly began to corrode and sizzle, leaving a hole and a fresh globule of blackish-green goop.

Macallister said they were acid shooters. The acid liquefies the leaf and the adult butterflies drink it. It was the only example he knew of in the animal kingdom where the young were responsible for providing their parents with food.

"Whoa!" I said.

"Ugh!" said Mhairie. "If you want me I'll be with the potami."

She had been very quiet since the story of my dad.

"The baby Selkie," I asked Macallister, "it was Mhairie, wasn't it?"

He nodded. "But she doesn't know."

"She's a smart seal," I said. "She'll figure it out. What happened to her dad?"

"Eaten by a killer whale."

The book she'd been reading was lying on the table. "A killer whale from Dwam?"

He shook his head. "Just a regular orca—about two years ago. He swam out too far alone. It happens. I try to help her mother as much as I can."

He said this too casually. I figured Mhairie's mother might be another reason he stayed on the island.

The sleepypotami had carried their dead hero down to Loch Snooze and were saying goodbye. They had covered his fur in mountain flowers and stood on their hind legs with heads bowed, Mhairie standing with them, as they pushed him into the water. He floated on his back for a few minutes then slowly sank, and the potami turned and plodded back up the hill.

The little potamus who had befriended me earlier wheeped excitedly to the others, who nodded and patted her. Then she jumped into my arms.

"That's Flims," Macallister said. "Both of her parents are dead and the whole group adopted her. Now she wants to stay with you."

"Wow!" I was overwhelmed. "OK then Flims, we're a team!"

Mhairie looked surprised and I think her nose was out of joint, but she'd get over it.

Macallister was right in his opinion that the denizens would not attack again that day. On the trek home I took comfort from the Blackflash in my pocket, the diary under my shirt, and the furry body of Flims riding on my shoulder. We had one scare when we disturbed a colony of rokroaches that went skittering under our feet in annoyance. We all jumped and then laughed in relief. Flims slipped down from my shoulder, snatched a few up and ate them, whooing with satisfaction. I was a bit shocked when Mhairie also shoved a couple in her mouth and crunched happily. Another reminder that she was *not actually human.*

The beetles were about an inch long and covered in grayish green lumps. Rocks—you guessed it—calcium carbonate rocks. So far, I knew about three species and *two different phyla* that used this same adaptation.

"It's like the island's recycling an idea," I said suddenly.

Malcolm shrugged, but I could see he was thinking about it.

"Anyway, they taste good," Mhairie grinned.

"You're an awesome possum," said Malcolm, to prove that he was not put-off by Mhairie eating insects.

"She's the real seal," I agreed.

She gave us both a look that could have stripped paint, but she was pleased.

I was glad to get home and looked forward to a peaceful evening with my dad's diary, but I didn't get it.

As I neared the open door of the living room I heard my mom say, "I'll be alright in a minute."

And my dad mumbled something I couldn't catch.

And then my mom again, "… shouldn't tell him until we know for sure."

"What's up?" I said brightly.

They both jumped, guiltily. My mom was lying back on the sofa. She was shivering, though trying not to, and her face was shock white with a sheen of sweat. My dad was holding her hand.

"What's wrong, Mom?"

She made an effort to laugh that would have been pathetic if it hadn't been terrifying.

"Oh, something I ate, I think," she said.

"Never eat mussels from an experimental farm," said my dad, in another unconvincing attempt at humor.

And they refused to admit that it might be more serious, which told me how worried they were.

They hadn't even noticed Flims.

I was sure now that Harry was trying to get to me through her. It made me more furious than the roktopus and the scrabs and the rokchiks put together. In my room I looked out at the night, which was peaceful and bright with stars.

"You want a piece of me? Come and get it, Darkman!" I yelled. "Just lay off my mom!"

I spent the night practicing—stabbing and slicing imaginary Harrys while Flims curled up on my bed, wheeping quietly until I dropped down beside her, exhausted, and fell into a thankfully dreamless sleep.

Chapter Six

The Acid Poop-Shooting Caterpillars of Doom

I woke next morning late and bleary eyed to a sunny day, Flims snuffling my left ear, and the unmistakable sound of my mother hurling in the bathroom.

Malcolm's mother, Maggie MacDodd, was too cheerfully making tea in the kitchen.

"Hi Flims!" she said. "Malcolm told me about her," she explained.

"Hey little guy!" my dad said. "Last night I thought he was a sweatshirt."

A fluffy, lavender pastel sweatshirt. Of mine. Of course he did.

"She's a little girl," I replied.

I rooted around in the fridge, not finding anything for Flims to eat. I would have to lay in a supply of daisies and fresh fish. In the meantime, she lolloped outside to snack on the large and overgrown yard. I grabbed a box of eggs and put a frying pan on the stove.

"Oh, please not now!" my mother begged.

I put the eggs back and opted for Chocoshreddies.

She and my dad were sitting at the table holding hands. My dad had not shaved and there were lines in his face where there had been none before. My mother could barely hold her head up.

"'Sup, Mom?" I spoke casually.

"Maggie and I are going shopping in Oban."

Of course they were. When you have been having nightmares and heaving for weeks and sometimes can't remember your name and you dread the smell of sunny side ups, it is quite natural to take a small boat across a choppy ocean on the spur of the moment for the thrill of examining hairy sweaters and thistles immortalized in plastic. With your doctor.

Also, she wore sweatpants and a T-shirt, which if you know my mom is just not realistic. A day on the town would normally mean an outfit with at least five different colors twisted together, ragged bits of silk and knitting, earrings like small lanterns, shoes that look like anything but, streamers, and possibly balloons.

OK, so I'm exaggerating. You get the idea.

There was no point insisting on being told why they were really going. There was a united front and I would have more luck tackling my dad when my mom and Maggie were gone. In any case, this solved my first problem of how to get her off the island.

I demanded to see them off at the boat dock.

As it turned out, they did not take a small boat across the choppy ocean. The DODO was flying them out in an army 'copter. For shopping. There just happened to be two free seats on a scheduled flight. Of course there were.

It this point, I actually think they realized that it wasn't realistic to expect me to swallow all of this, but they were too far along with the deception to go back on it now.

"Angus," my mom said, "I know we've worried you, but I really am alright and I'll see you in a day or two." And that did make me feel a bit better—she sounded more like herself now that she was leaving.

Macallister had advised us not to try to convince any adults of the existence of Dwam since they wouldn't believe it anyway, or if they did, they would want to investigate making things even worse. But given my mom's condition, I had to at least try to convince my dad that the island was bad for her.

I said on the way back in the jeep, "You know how we were all dizzy and sick and having weird dreams?"

"Right, we had jet lag."

"I think it's worse than that."

"Maybe a virus."

"I think the dreamons are really strong here and they're making Mom sick."

"Your mother will be fine Angus." I could see the muscles in his cheek contracting, like caterpillars under his skin.

"If she comes back, it's going to get worse."

"That's *enough!*"

I was shocked at the way he spoke to me. My dad almost never raises his voice. Not even when I broke my face and my Quicksilver in the illegal surf.

As I believe I have mentioned before, my dad is not your common or garden-variety dad. Usually, he'd be all over the idea that particle-wave-particles floating around in bad-guy clouds could get into a person's head and make the person toss her breakfast. That he refused to discuss the possibility meant two things: (1) he was too worried about my mom to theorize, and (2) he thought he already knew what was wrong with her. None of this made me feel any better.

I tried to calm down and focus on the plan we had worked out with Macallister. In theory, it was pretty simple. It was

Malcolm's and my job to figure out what the DODO was doing to strengthen Dwam, then we would somehow stop them from doing it, and finally we would destroy Murky Harry and the denizens and dissipate the Dwam energy that had already built up. No sweat.

I wished I had paid more attention to my parents' work before. "So, how is your work going, Dad?" was not something I asked too often. But he was relieved to have something else to talk about.

It turned out that they were running a big experiment that day and our house was one of the test sites. The deal was that this one computer program might be picking up bursts of energy that did not just register as noise, but as information that the program might be able to translate. The experiment was to run the program from different computers at different places on the island. If they all recorded the same burst at the same time, that would be a success and they might even be able to use the intensity at different places to pinpoint the source. Then if they could translate it, they might be able to understand it and broadcast it to other computers—and maybe even brains.

How great would that be?

Malcolm had already gone with his dad to the DODO where they were coordinating the effort. Strictly speaking, he was not supposed to be allowed in there, but the rules on the island were pretty relaxed and so long as his dad vouched for him, the security guards looked the other way. He was really well known in there and helped his dad quite a bit, which would be really useful when we figured out how to sabotage the DODO's plans.

My dad had a desktop in his study and a laptop in the kitchen, both running DODO/DREAMON/17. At the same time a different computer in their bedroom was running

DODO/DREAMON/24, which was not expected to pick up a translatable signal.

All three computers were registering occasional symbols and numbers. "The usual background noise," my dad told his colleagues over the phone.

After that, not a lot happened for a while. My dad started a few conversations with me about surfing and where did I think I would like to go to college, but kept drifting into depressed silence, thinking about Mom. I went into my room with Flims to read my dad's (meaning Dad 1's) diary. At the beginning there was a lot of stuff about his PhD thesis and how much he loved Mom 1 and how excited he was to be having a baby. It was hard to read because I love Dad 2, but I wish I hadn't missed out on Dad 1, who seemed to have been a neat guy. Same thing with Mom 1 and Mom 2. I figured I'd just have to live with this and would spend more time on it later.

In the meantime, I flipped to the end of the diary and the last couple of weeks of his life. He had written a lot about what the Blackflash could do. To stay focused, I phoned Mhairie and persuaded her to come over and help me practice.

She was frosty on the cell and when she turned up, her stiff shoulders began to relax when Flims clambered into her arms and nuzzled her face.

"Thanks for coming," I said, meaning it. She shrugged, but was definitely thawing out. We walked out into the garden to hang out and absorb all of the troubling events of the past few days.

Our cottage was on the westernmost edge of the village of Nap, a bit apart from the others, and it had been the keeper's cottage of a walled garden. In the past, there had been more people (or Selkies) here than there were now, which explained why there were empty houses available for scientists, and at some time they had taken the trouble to create this garden. I guessed that regular people had built the garden—maybe even one of the heroes from a couple hundred years ago—because Selkies would have been more likely to build something to do with the sea rather than the land. Mhairie said she didn't know.

When you walked out of our front door you were in a leafy lane that led to other houses, shops, and Mhairie's mother's cafe. When you left by the back door you were in another world. It was one of the things that made me wonder how I'd lucked out (before I was crushed and poisoned and battered by semi-precious stones and snacked on by infant crustaceans).

The garden was the length of a football pitch and was surrounded by a stone wall about ten feet high with a gate in one side that was my dad's shortcut to the DODO. There was a deep, low-walled pond at the back. The surface of the pond was covered with chillypads—tough, flat, green circles that generate cold and are sparkley with ice crystals, even in summer.

There were trees of all kinds including apple, cherry and weeping willow, with a bunch of small birds and animals—some familiar and some that were only found on the Snugglays—living in the branches. There were plants that I had never seen before either. My favorites were the tripodecons, which looked like short green windmills with three big flat seedpods that spun in the wind until they flew off to break on the ground, spilling out their big, soft, green seeds. You could eat these like soybeans and they could be dried into a snack food that was really popular with the visiting scientists. These snacks were also one of Mhairie's family's sidelines.

There were winding paths half buried in grass and wildflowers with scattered statues and fountains created in the island's special colors of purple, green and marbley white. The sculptures depicted the rare inhabitants of the islands, including one of a Selkie half out of her skin, a roktopus with most of its tentacles chipped off, and a mommy rokchik with fluffy babies balanced on the edge of a tiled birdbath. In the center of the garden was a six-sided gazebo—which is like an open-sided, freestanding room where you can sit and be outside and be sheltered from the weather at the same time. It had stone pillars and a shingled roof with marble benches and a table inside that still showed how beautifully it had been tiled in blue and white with gold accents.

Close to the gazebo was a stand of thornegos, which Flims considered a sublime dining experience.

"No Flims! You'll get thorns in your paws." I dragged her away from the plants. They had tall, woody stems with balloon-like fruit covered all over in sharp spikes. The fruit started out very pink and matured to gold and as the balloons swelled the spikes grew longer and curved over. When they were ripe, the spikes punctured the balloons and out spilled a rich harvest of golden seeds. But these were not ripe yet. Flims wheeped in disappointment and contented herself with tripodecon seeds.

I like the Blackflash best as a blade. It feels comfortable in my hand, and I can slash and slice with good precision. I learned to control the length, so it can be a short dagger or a longer sword.

I can also throw a long beam, like Macallister had done to kill the rokchiks. I read that Dad 1 hated the kind of mind-pushing you need to do this and I have to admit, I am with him on that one. It feels a lot like throwing up.

"It's a necessary skill," Mhairie said, like I shouldn't be complaining.

"I just hope I won't need it too often." I had to rest for a bit until the queasiness subsided.

Then there are the rapid pulses that shoot out of the weapon like balls of wavy air. These don't feel anywhere near as bad as the long beam, and I could see that they'd be really useful against a bunch of small Dwam denizens, so I practiced them hard. This made Mhairie actually laugh. According to her I lunged my head forward with every wavy air ball release.

"You look like a chicken!"

I laughed with her, relieved that we were good again, and hen-toe stepped while shooting the pulses, saying, "Buck buck!" to make her laugh more.

Flims and I walked her a little way down the road. The evening was warm and smelled of fruit and flowers that the sun had been cooking. Beside the next house along the road stood a pickup truck containing Macallister, some of Macallister's furniture and equipment, and Mhairie's mom, Sylvy (who was almost as beautiful as Mhairie). She was helping him move in.

"Change of scenery!" said Macallister by way of explanation. "Bit lonely up on the hill."

We helped them carry the caterpillar tank and some of the bigger pieces inside and then left them to it.

"Mac and your mom seem pretty thick." I said to Mhairie.

"Whatever," she gave her usual *don't care* shrug, but I could see that she was thinking about this as the corners of her mouth were going up. Just as well. I wouldn't give much for Macallister's chances against opposition from Mhairie, though I guessed her mom was a pretty strong character too.

From my own point of view, I was certainly glad to have him next door. I told him to come over later and meet my dad.

We had chili and rice for dinner and I tried to keep Dad company, but I knew he was fretting because the cell phones were cutting out again and he couldn't call my mom. Then a *ting!* from both of the Program 17 computers made him jump and knock over our game of Monopoly, which hadn't been going well anyway because Flims wanted to eat the money.

Lines of 0s and 1s were running across both screens, faster and faster until they were more or less a blur. My dad ran into the bedroom, where Program 24 was picking up, "Junk! Yes!" he yelled triumphantly, grabbing his phone again.

The phone would not work at all.

"I have to go to the compound," Dad said, but I could tell he didn't want to leave me figuring that he would probably be pulling an all-nighter.

"It's OK," I told him, "I'll bring my sleeping bag and crash in the lounge."

My first clue that something was very wrong was Flims wheeping in panic and trying to climb inside my shirt.

The second was when we opened the door. The mellow evening had turned sinister and cold. The fragrance of sun-warmed fruit and flowers was replaced by a smell like old garbage. That familiar circular wind was swooping around, howling. The wind chimes jingled in alarm.

"Dad, maybe we should stay inside," I said, but he was halfway down the garden and heading for the gate. I caught up to him and grabbed his sleeve. "Dad!"

And the third clue was the two humongous green caterpillars that oozed out of the bushes and squelched in our direction.

They were four feet in diameter and twenty feet long, the color of wilted spinach, and covered in foot-long waving spikes, which I figured were their version of sensory hairs. Their bodies were made up of about twenty segments and they moved like rippling green slime. The back segments pushed the front end forwards, and then the front segments pulled the back ones. They probably didn't need legs, but had nine pairs, all with hooks on the feet. In regular caterpillars the front three pairs are mainly for grabbing things—like food. They had six eyes on each side of their heads, but with all that sensory equipment they probably didn't need them much either. These denizens were going to be difficult to disable.

Oh, yeah. The most developed part of their bodies were their mouths—soggy, black, dripping holes under mandibles like meat cleavers, which they showed-off proudly as they reared up, waggling their front three pairs of legs and chomping in anticipation.

"What the heck?" said my dad, frozen to the spot.

One of them surged across the front of the house, completely blocking the front door, and twisted the front part of its body menacingly towards us. The other one slid into position in front of the gate, trapping us in the garden.

I pulled my dad out of his freeze and he and I ran to the gazebo. It wasn't great protection, but better than nothing.

"Angus!" It was Macallister on the path outside. We could see him through the gate.

The second caterpillar's upper body twisted towards him, hissing with feet clawing the air.

He was trying to draw the giant larva away from us, but instead it spat a white rope at him—liquid silk from its spinnerets, that dripped over Macallister and then hardened, encasing him in a sticky cocoon. He managed to keep his head free but his arms and legs were trapped and he slumped against the gatepost, immobile. The caterpillar didn't waste any more time on him. It advanced on my dad and me.

I had left the Blackflash in my bedroom. I could see it through the open window in the side of the house. Macallister saw me looking and figured it out.

"Flims! Get the Blackflash!" shouted Macallister.

She wheeped in terror and cuddled tighter inside my shirt. But she was our only shot.

"Flims!" I said urgently. "You have to get the Blackflash. The Blackflash, Flims!"

"Wheep!" her fur was standing up in spikes, the whole of her little body trembling.

"Go!" I threw her out of the gazebo.

"Wheep! Wheep!" She landed just under the open window. She looked back at me, terrified and undecided, then made up her mind and leaped up through the window.

My dad had stopped asking "*What the Heck?*" and got with the program. There were tarps folded up in a corner that could be hung to keep the rain out. We got one up just as the caterpillar came within spitting distance. We heard it hiss furiously as the liquid silk thudded into the tarp like a jet from a garden hose and dripped down in a heavy rain. We got another tarp up, but it wasn't going to help us for long.

The larva was too big to squeeze between the pillars that held the gazebo up. It also did not try banging its head against them, which might have given us some time to escape. We heard it slither up the tarp and over the roof and down the other side, so it was draped over the structure. We got the third tarp in place just in time to block the white jet that it aimed at us.

Then it started to squeeze, contracting the segments of its huge, muscular body. Blue, white and gold tiles rained down from the roof, and the pillars started to buckle. My dad grabbed me and tried to protect me with his body as the gazebo continued to crumble.

"Whoo!" Flims slipped under the edge of a tarp and scrambled into my arms. She had the Blackflash. Relief flooded through me as my hand gripped the cool, rubbery cylinder.

I lifted the tarp and pushed out the Blackflash blade. The back end of the caterpillar with its stumpy legs waving was in front of me framed between two stone pillars. With a swipe, I sliced off the back five segments, which liquefied and dripped into a putrid green pool. We ran out of the structure. The rest of the caterpillar was still lying over the roof, the head end dangling down, twisting and thrashing in pain and fury.

Before it could spray me I lunged at it, driving my blade between its eyes. It froze, transfixed, then shock waves ran through its body from the head backwards until finally it decomposed into a disgusting slime that oozed over the roof of the building and trickled down the pillars.

"What is that thing?" demanded my dad.

"No time! Run!"

The second caterpillar left its guard post in front of the door and pulsed our way. This time I didn't let it get close, but pushed a long beam out of the Blackflash directly into the chomping maw. For a second the creature lit up from within and I saw the slippery black sides of its gut. Then it expanded like an overblown balloon and broke into a mosaic of fragments that hovered in the air for a moment, then slimified and splatted on the paving.

A wave of nausea broke over me and I stumbled.

"Angus, come on!" Now my dad was dragging me over the sticky, slippery mess toward the cottage door.

"We have to get Macallister!" I managed to shout.

"I will!" My dad ran to the gate and pulled Macallister into the garden. I got some strength back and between us we dragged him in his chrysalis into the cottage and slammed the door. As we ran, I had the impression of a thin, caped figure under the willows.

The wind was still howling. "It isn't over!" Macallister yelled.

I looked out of the large back window. Another caterpillar seethed out of the bushes, then the window frame filled with a bristling green face and salivating mouthparts.

I aimed the Blackflash and shot another long beam. It felt like a punch in the gut and I fell back against the wall.

The face disappeared. But I knew I hadn't hit it. It had simply dropped out of range below the windowsill.

Through the window I could see the tail end lift up, curl over, and shoot a volley of black gobs the size of beach balls. The window glass melted on first contact and dripped like transparent candle wax over the sill to solidify in glass icicles. One or two poops whacked the window frame; the white paint blackened and blistered, then the wood itself was eaten away in wet, ragged, smoking bites.

Most of the giant acid poops whizzed clean through the window and hit various places in the room. A couple hit the front door, burning two dinner plate-sized holes in it. One hit the laptop on the table. Bang! It shorted then its plastic melted into a twisted, gray pile. One hit an armchair, corroding through to the foam padding, and one splatted on Macallister's cocoon.

"No!" I yelled, diving for him, but the chrysalis did him some good. The evil smelling substance ran off it without harming him. Dad and I dragged him under the table and the three of us waited for the barrage to stop.

"When it looks in to see what happened, you can get it," Macallister said. "Keep very still, it'll think it got us."

We froze and waited. Eventually, the hairy green face appeared, twitching, and the monster, not sensing us started to squeeze into the room. I flinched but Macallister shook his head warning me to wait.

The caterpillar's front end elongated as it overflowed through the window frame and spilled onto the floor.

"Now! Go!"

My dad grabbed for me, but I slipped his grasp and leapt to the window. The caterpillar spat and the white stuff coated my legs and stuck my jeans together, but my blade was out and as I went down on my knees I sliced, cutting the creature in half.

The front end fell into the room. The back end was stuck in the window frame and spilled its intestines onto the floor in a steaming pile.

Slowly, everything evaporated along with the heavy stink in the air, which was replaced again by the summer evening's fragrance and a delicate breeze.

It was over.

My dad was still on his hands and knees where he had lost his grip on me. "What just happened?" he said.

I ripped the stiff material that bound my ankles. It tore like canvas. The caterpillar silk had not disappeared with the caterpillars. I figured this was a bad sign of the Dwam denizens' increasing hold on reality.

"Lads!" said Macallister from under the table. "Can I have some help over here?"

I brought out the kitchen scissors to cut him free.

"Watch where you're putting those, laddie!" he warned.

"Will. Somebody. Please. Tell me. What. Just. Happened?" My dad seemed to be almost in shock.

I looked at Macallister, who shrugged. "This is going to take some liquid courage. Do you have any whisky?" he said.

My parents kept a bottle of Johnnie Walker for when somebody had a bad cold. After the second shot the color returned to their faces, and after the fourth or fifth my dad and Macallister were good buddies. I was only allowed hot chocolate.

"Are those things native to this island?" demanded my dad.

"Well, yes, in a manner of speaking." Macallister spun him some tale about sea serpents that came onto land during storms, which he reasoned would be alright because my dad wouldn't remember this anyway and he wouldn't be able to talk to any of the other scientists this night because communications were still out. Even though the Dwam energy had died down, all the other DODO people were trying to call and email each other about their experiment, so the wireless tower was jammed.

Flims and I fell asleep on the charred sofa, listening to the comforting voice of Macallister's story telling and my dad grilling him for details.

The last thing I remembered before I drifted off was the image of Murky Harry under the willow trees, snarling.

Chapter Seven

The Twisting of The Twelve O'clock Ferry

I woke to the smell of French toast for the first time since my mom started getting sick. I was lying on the partly destroyed sofa under a stripey blanket and Flims. Macallister and the silk cocoons were gone. My dad was cooking breakfast and humming a mixture of *The Star-Spangled Banner* and *Scotland The Brave*, wearing an apron with a picture of a small furry animal that was supposed to be a haggis on it.

Warm air and sunlight streamed through the ragged hole that used to be a window.

"I let you sleep," he said. "That freakoid storm did a number on our house. We were actually struck by lightning."

This was his explanation for the burn holes in the door and the charred walls and furniture. So he really didn't remember anything.

"Do you want syrup on your French? You know, the French call this *Le Pain Perdu*, which literally means, "lost bread.""

I glanced out at the garden that looked steamrollered, which was more or less what had happened.

"Rain beat everything flat," said my dad. "I guess this is what they call *weather*."

"Tell me about it," I said.

He grinned, "The experiment worked."

I realized he must be itching to get to the compound, but he hadn't wanted me to wake up alone.

"That's great," I said, and meant it, because now we knew for sure what was causing the rise of Dwam. Program DODO/ DREAMON/17. Next on our official agenda was to shut that program down.

Next on my personal agenda was to stop my mom from coming back to the island before we shut the program down and got rid of Murky Harry.

"And," my dad said, grinning, "your mom's coming back today!"

"She can't!"

He pointed his eggy spatula at me, "Don't start that again."

"This island is making her sick."

He sat down and put his elbows on the table, looking at me with that man-to-man stare that meant I was being taken seriously but was not going to get what I wanted.

"Angus, I know we weren't completely straight with you and probably that was wrong. We were just really worried and, you know, not sure how to handle it all." He waved the spatula and bits of egg flew off and stuck to a patch of blistered paint on the wall.

"However," he continued, "she's had some tests. They were perfect. They gave her a vitamin shot and she feels great."

"If she comes back here she'll feel terrible again."

"I spoke to her ten minutes ago. She's fabulous."

"Shouldn't she at least wait until she's been fabulous for, like, a couple of days? Just in case?"

"And miss the greatest moment of her life? This is the big one for us, Angus. Try to understand."

This was as close as my dad had ever come to expressing disappointment in my lack of aptitude for Advanced Theoretical Physics. There was no chance of me talking him round now.

After breakfast, I talked to my mom on the phone, with the same result.

"My mom wouldn't listen to me either," I told the others when we gathered in Macallister's new kitchen for a council of war. "Says she blames herself for not being straight with me and making me paranoid, and she's going to make it up to me. She's so happy that if the house caught on fire she'd probably say it needed redecorating anyway.

"In fact," I said, thinking about it and remembering the acid poop damage in the kitchen, "she probably will say that."

"And," I admitted, "at this point, I am paranoid. I heard my dad on the phone saying, 'Ninety-eight percent sure it's OK, but we're not going to tell him 'till we're absolutely sure,' and my mind's writing screenplays with it."

"She must have had some kind of scan," Malcolm reasoned, "to get an answer that quickly. And now they're waiting for confirmatory blood work."

I looked at him. "Cheers, buddy. That helps."

Mhairie, who was eating kippers and dried seaweed, kicked him under the table. "You know Angus," she said, "maybe your mom did just need a vitamin shot. And if she's strong and happy, not with jet lag, it'll be harder for Harry to get his claws into."

"Thanks Mhairie," I said, and meant it, although I wished she'd hurry up and finish her smelly breakfast. She picked up a kipper skeleton and started delicately nibbling off the yellow flakes that were still clinging. My stomach turned over.

Maybe the island was getting to me. "Do you mind if I open a window?"

She grumbled and pulled her sweater closer.

"Whatever," said Macallister, "the best way we can help your mom—and the rest of the human race—is to develop a robust plan of attack."

Macallister looked none the worse for wear for his encounter with the caterpillar straitjacket. I saw that he had some pieces of the material and had been examining them under the microscope. I figured it was a bad sign that the stuff was still in existence. His tank of regular acid poop-shooting caterpillars was on his worktable. Some were still chomping and shooting acid poop, but a couple had already cocooned themselves and were lying in their thick white shiny cases on the floor under the rhubarb leaves, jerking occasionally, so he had material to make comparisons with.

"Their grip on reality is strengthening," he confirmed, "but we knew that would happen. We have no time to lose."

Flims was fascinated by the caterpillars and I think wanted to eat them. She balanced on the edge of the tank, swinging her paw inside until she lost her footing and fell in, wheeping indignantly. Her soft, pink fur was sticky with splotches of the black-green slime, which was thankfully no longer corrosive.

"Ach, Flims!" said Macallister. He picked her out and put her in the sink where she played happily under the tap while the rest of us got down to business.

"I have a plan already," Malcolm said.

"The Selkies are with us," Mhairie picked seaweed out of her teeth with a fish bone. "The network's alerted."

Macallister said the Selkies would be an invaluable force. Although their numbers were down—a bunch of them having been killed twelve years ago fighting with my dad—this was the first time that the Dwam denizens would face seal people who remembered what it was like to fight them.

I had to admit that Malcolm had thought things through. There was no question that he and Macallister were the strategic brains of the outfit. First, we had to delete all copies of DODO/DREAMON/17.

"But there's no point doing it willy nilly," Malcolm said.

"Willy nilly?"

"Just pay attention."

The master file of the program was stored in the DODO's main grid, which was on the other island, Great Snugglay. We had to take this and its backups out first. If we deleted any of the downloaded copies that were on people's hard drives without doing that, when they found that their copy didn't work they'd just download it again from the mainframe.

"Do you not think they'll notice that it's missing?" Mhairie asked drily, chewing on her seaweed.

Malcolm had been waiting for this. He tried not to look smug, but his lips trembled and he couldn't help darting a glance at Macallister. "We'll replace it with something else. Something that doesn't work."

"Like DODO/DREAMON/24," I said, catching on.

"Precisely!" Trying to prevent himself from grinning, he stuffed his mouth with toast and marmalade, which resulted in a rain of crumbs and a gooey orange mess that festered all over his face.

Mhairie shrugged, "Not bad," and passed him a piece of kitchen roll.

He cleaned his face, which was now red under the marmalade, and he recovered quickly as he went on with his plan.

"To do this, we have to go to Great Snugglay and get into the mainframe room to swap the files and backups. I have all the security codes, but I can't just walk in there in broad daylight with nobody asking questions. I'll need to sneak in at night. That's going to be the easy part."

"There's a hard part?"

"Then we have to swap the programs on the ancillary network at the DODO compound here on Little Snugglay, and then on all the individual hard drives. That program has been downloaded to thirty-six laptop computers. My plan is to cause a minor problem, like with email that they have to bring their laptops in for us to fix. I often help my dad with that stuff so I should be able to get to every laptop and swap the files."

Mhairie said, "Why don't you just engineer a virus that replaces 17 with 24 as soon as a laptop logs on to the network? You could make that spread through email."

Malcolm looked at her in actual shock. Another piece of toast fell out of his mouth.

"That's a good idea, Mhairie," Macallister said, respectfully.

"Well, I did think of it," said Malcolm, "but the truth is that I don't have time. Hacking is painstaking work, you know."

Mhairie rolled her eyes.

"I could be working on that," said Macallister. "Not that there's any guarantee, but I could have a crack."

So it was decided. Macallister would work on the virus, with Malcolm's help when we were not breaking and entering. Malcolm set him up with some basic information and he got started right away. Malcolm and I walked down to the Slumber Strait to scope it out and plan our attack while Mhairie went home to get the boat that we needed to cross it.

The strait was about 100 feet across, a stretch of purpley blue green, gently lapping water between the shingles of the two islands. The colors were from the amethyst and chalcedony on the seabed. The roktopi would be down there, minding their business of raising babies.

"We have a perfect right to be here," Malcolm said, "but let's not draw attention to ourselves."

There was a grove of mangroids—big, salt-loving, gnarly trees with a complicated root system that grow close to the ocean—so we hung out there to wait for Mhairie. Under the mangroids was a stand of thornegos. Almost ripe.

"Whoo!" Flims jumped down from my shoulder excitedly, snuffling and flapping her paws at the spiky fruit. On some of them, the balloons were golden and swollen, the spikes bent over almost piercing the rind.

"Wheep! Wheep!" Flims begged, and as we watched, the pod seemed to inflate a bit more, then made contact with the spikes and split open with a soft, ripe pfft! A rush of golden seeds spilled out and the spiky skin flew off in the light breeze to float on the surface of the strait.

"Whoo!" Flims crowed in triumph, stuffing her mouth with the rich harvest and rolling on the ground. First thornego seeds of the year. I ate a few, and had to admit they were pretty delicious. I felt a lot better than usual as well.

"Do these have some drug in them?" I asked Malcolm.

"Not categorized—yet," he said. "There is some Selkie legend that they give you courage."

Courage. That I could use. Not poisonous, anyway. I kept chewing. Looked at my watch. It was 12:30.

"They'll be almost at Mull," I said.

Obviously, he knew I was talking about our moms. He was too good a friend to try cheering me up.

"Macallister's right, Angus. The best way to help your mum is to destroy our Prince of Darkness."

As if Harry himself had heard that, the light dimmed. The purpley, blue-green water switched to gray, its gentle surface now frothy with fragmented waves and the chill, circular wind swooped around, looking for something to hurt.

"Oh, man," I said.

"Here we go," muttered Malcolm.

Dropping her seeds, Flims jumped under my shirt.

The Blackflash was solid in my right hand, my other arm protecting Flims. Malcolm had taken to carrying an expandable steel pointer that he had sharpened at the tip. It was light and very strong, and I had to admit it made a pretty effective makeshift weapon.

We stood back to back, covering the 360° around us, waiting.

And we kept waiting—knees bent, weapon arms tensed, jumping at every tiny sound.

After five minutes, Malcolm said, "He's psyching us out, just wearing us down and sapping our energy. He can keep this up forever with no denizens at all."

He was right. However much I dreaded the denizens, I'd rather have something to fight than this war of nerves.

"Any suggestions?"

"Well, there's no point yelling at him," Malcolm said, which told me what he, like me, really wanted to do.

There was no safe place. If we went in the open, something would swoop from above; if we stayed in the shade, something would crawl from the trees.

"Let's go back to Macallister. He might know what to do."

"Shhh!"

I heard it too, and it was almost a relief—a low, grumbling, moaning sound with quiet splashes, coming closer, not wanting to be heard. Something was coming down the strait, pushing water ahead of it—something that was big enough to eat us.

We stood shoulder to shoulder and faced it through the fog. I can't speak for Malcolm, but my nerves were stretched to breaking. Gradually, a shape emerged from the thick white air. It was huge, bulky, the size of a...

"Owp! Owp!"

A motorboat appeared from the fog with a small seal splashing alongside.

Malcolm and I both laughed at the release of tension, momentarily forgetting the signs of Dwam.

"Are we glad to see you!"

But Mhairie's face was as gray as the air around it and stole the warmth of her welcome.

The seal beside her was her little brother, Elpy. "Owp!" he barked again, and he had brought bad news.

"There's a roktopus," she said. "It's attacking the twelve o'clock ferry."

Half an hour later, al three of us were in the little boat on the open sea, heading to do battle with the roktopus.

"Can you go any faster?" I was standing at the helm, trying to push the boat through the choppy water. I wasn't scared just furious, and I felt like I could handle any monster that threatened my mother if I could just get to it. I think my bravado had a lot to do with the thornego seeds.

"This is as good as it gets!"

I knew I owed her already, but patience just wasn't in my repertoire right then. Her little brother was still leaping through the waves.

"Elpy, go home!" Malcolm yelled.

Mhairie looked. "Elpy!" She twisted between looking down at him and keeping the boat on course. "Home, Elpy!"

Elpy was seven years old. I am not sure what that meant for his seal self, but he still had some of his white baby fur and was clearly too small to be out in a sea like this, much less heading to a date with disaster.

Despite the scolding, he continued to owp joyfully as he galloped through the heaving surf.

I had been acting like I was the only one with skin in this game. Now, both of my best friends had family members in mortal danger. Not to mention the threat to their own lives.

"Elpy, go *home!*" I joined in.

We could see the bulk of the Island of Mull now and the closer we got, the grayer the sky was, the higher the swell of the ocean, the colder and more bitter was the air. Needles of horizontal rain whipped our faces, the wind hardly broken by the Plexiglas screen in the prow. The sea gave a huge lurch, pitching the boat up so it almost lost contact with the water. At the same time, it tossed Elpy into the air.

"Owp!" he shouted gleefully.

The boat fell back before Elpy did. On the way down, I reached out and looped my arm around his little body and scooped him into the boat.

"Owp! Owp!" He was furious and slapped me with his tail.

"Take the helm!" yelled Mhairie at Malcolm. She put her face down close to Elpy's twitching whiskers and snarled at him in seal speak. Whatever she said, as she explained to her mother later, 'It settled his hash.'

Elpy whimpered and hung his sleek little head. Then he scampered under a tarp at the back of the deck and reappeared a couple of seconds later as a dark, curly headed second-grader in jeans and a windbreaker.

I think there must be a Selkie code that gets drummed into them from infancy, that no matter what the circumstances they never let a human see them change.

It was now way too rough for Elpy to be in the ocean. He was safer in the boat. Seeing our faces, he finally realized how grave the situation was. His brown eyes were almost as big as they had been when he was a seal and his little face was peaked. We pushed him and Flims under the tarp at the back of the boat where there was a partly covered area, and the two of them huddled together making small, whimpering sounds.

The ocean pushed us on almost faster than the propeller. Mull was behind us now, and there was the ferry—a majestic white, two-story boat, shining against the gray, with a blue stripe highlighting her name: *The Viking Queen*. She pitched and tossed on disorganized waves.

Her bow and her stern—by which I mean her front end and her back end—were gripped and squeezed by the sixteen, eighty-foot tentacles of two massive, sparkling, green and purple roktopi.

The tentacles slid over The Viking Queen's hull, strengthening their grip, and one of the monsters twisted left while the other twisted right. Clearly, they intended to rip the boat apart.

The tiny dark bodies of terrified human beings ran and slid up and down the deck and several tumbled over the side into the roiling water with each lurch of the monster cephalopods. And strolling on the deck orchestrating the mayhem was a dark, malevolent, man-sized figure. Harry!

"Mom!" "Mum!" said Malcolm and I together.

The knobbly head-bodies of the denizens were half out of the water and even from this distance, I could see that there was something different about them. Their huge, vulnerable eyes were not blue and squashy like before, but bumpy and reflective, like the sockets were filled with large bubbles. What it was— screens made up of lumps of clear quartz protected the eyes. Not so vulnerable, then. Vision couldn't have been that great, but I guess when your main goal in life is to rip apart a boat the size of a hotel you don't need 20/20.

The water between the ferry and us was filled with little propeller boats like ours, and sleek dark heads bobbing in the surf. Selkies. The Network out in force. As we watched, the seals grabbed the humans in the water, gripping clothing in their teeth, and hauled them to the little boats where their kinfolk in human form pulled them to relative safety.

Meantime, green and purple boulders were crashing down around them.

We could steer for one of the monsters, and I could zap it with the Blackflash. They looked pretty strong, but eventually I'd dissolve it. Problem was that in the meantime the other one could take me out from behind with the flip of a tentacle. I wasn't sure, but I also suspected that the roktopi's reach might be longer than I could throw a beam with my weapon.

I looked at Malcolm. "Any ideas?" I yelled above the din, not really expecting much, but he surprised me.

"Actually," he yelled back, "I do have a plan!"

A minute later, Mhairie fixed us both with a commanding stare. "Keep Elpy on this boat! Unless it sinks!"

So that was clear enough. Then she slipped over the side, bobbed up again as a sleek gray head, and streamed through the chop to organize the other seals.

The plan was military genius. The Selkies powered their boats straight for the roktopi, one after another, and with a second before impact they set the boats to spin, so that the propellers hit the monsters right where the closest tentacle attached to the head-body. Meantime, the Selkies slipped over the side as people, flashed away under the waves and bobbed up again as seals at a safer distance.

The first boats didn't do much damage, but they did goad the denizens into flinging some rocks, exposing more vulnerable flesh that the propellers of the next boats could cut through like a steak knife through—well, not butter, but maybe rubber.

One huge amethyst crashed into a tiny craft, smashing it to splinters while its occupant jumped ship and reappeared, sleek, gray and whiskered, none the worse for wear.

Others were not so lucky. Some of the brave seal people, stunned and bleeding from flying gems, were dragged into boats and lay there twitching, while others sank and did not resurface—gone for good.

"Hooo! Hooo!" The roktopi bellowed like malignant foghorns, and the stench of singed calamari rose over the smell of the sea as ruined boats finally chewed tentacles clean through, leaving ragged, smoking stumps that dripped green gunk. The monsters shrieked again in pain and rage, but kept hold of The Viking Queen.

The sawn-off tentacles were easily eighty feet long, each like a huge, blind sea serpent, not slowed down at all by being severed from their bodies. If anything, they were more vigorous. One of them jackknifed onto the deck of the ferry where it whipped and twisted, knocking more terrified people into the ocean. The other came snaking through the water, heading for our boat.

Malcolm grabbed my shoulders. "It's up to you now, Angus. Only the Blackflash can inactivate the tentacles!"

Inactivate the tentacles. Right. I didn't wait for the thing to reach us. It would have to be a long beam, much as I hate them. I braced myself against the hull and threw one out of the Blackflash into the path of the monstrous sidewinder. Where the Blackflash beam hit the water it shimmered, a golden glow in the howling grayness that spread along the rocky green and purple muscle of the tentacle, freezing its motion. A ripple of light flowed through the tentacle from tip to ragged base, and then another, each higher than the first. We heard the enormous muscle hum, low and deep like the string of a huge guitar, until *twang,* it burst in a shower of light and rocks that popped out of existence before they hit the sea.

As I believe I have said already, I hate those long beams. I slumped, exhausted, and then I actually did toss my *pain perdu* over the side of the boat. It was lost bread now, alright.

When I lifted my face, Malcolm was screaming into it. Clearly there were more essential tasks that only the Blackflash could do, and when I looked beyond him, my empty stomach lurched again.

The Selkies had been busy. Four more ragged anacondas were humping towards us through the sea. Meantime, the first was still lashing on the ferry deck, and the remainders of the roktopi, each now with five tentacles, were not disabled in the slightest—only more angry than before. They shrieked and twisted in opposite directions, and the hull of The Viking Queen screamed and began to splinter. I couldn't see any more people on the deck, although there were plenty in the water.

Then, around the side of the ferry, I saw lifeboats filled with survivors heading for the mainland. So some of them would make it. I prayed that our mothers were on one of those boats.

I felt a rush of new strength and aimed the Blackflash at the closest tentacle. It glowed and rippled like the first, then the light waves ran through it until it exploded in the same shower of purple, green and gold.

I dry-heaved again, steadied myself, and got ready for the next.

Too late—it was on our boat, its tip snaking over the side like a deadly creeper. It flicked, almost casually, and swept Flims and Elpy, still huddled under the tarp, over the side and into that roiling sea of death.

"Nooo!" I screamed.

Malcolm grabbed Elpy's hand and clung for a moment, but the wind and waves pulled the little boy and the sleepypotamus under.

I pushed the Blackflash into a blade. Instantly, I felt stronger, complete. It was like an extension of my arm. "Yaaah!" I yelled, driving the tip of the blade into the tip of the tentacle and slicing upwards. The huge muscle split over my weapon, opening like a zipper, the two halves peeling away to dissolve in a sparkling shower.

With no time to rest, the next two were slithering over the side.

I chopped them up together into sections, like carrots on a chopping board, and they were gone.

More were on the way, but these I made short work of, slicing and dicing.

As I finished off number sixteen, we heard the death cry of The Viking Queen as she finally tore into two ragged pieces and swiftly sank.

Finally, only the two roktopus head-bodies were left, bobbing like giant green and purple grisly eyeballs. They spat their store of black poison, polluting the water before they sank, dissolving as they went.

Dwam had dissipated. The gray in the air melted away to reveal a clear sky and sun sparkling on gentle blue water. The sea, now calm, was littered with floating wreckage from the ferry and the smaller boats, with humans desperately splashing and seals struggling to pull them into the few boats that were still sea worthy.

"Malcolm, the toxin! Get the people into the boats! Remember the Selkies are immune!"

I figured we had an hour tops to get the humans out of the water and to the Oban Infirmary before they lost the ability to breathe. I scanned the water desperately for Elpy and Flims, but there was no little pink head, no little baby seal head. Elpy might survive, though there was no guarantee. Flims, probably not. They were both so little and defenseless.

It had been my job to defend them.

I tried not to think about them, or my mother and Malcolm's mom, as we focused on the mechanical task of pulling people out of the water.

We grabbed a little blond haired girl and boy who were clinging to a piece of The Viking Queen's blue stripe and hauled them in, then a woman who was screaming, "My babies!" who turned out to be their mother. They were already losing control of their arms and legs, though that might have been from cold and exhaustion.

A seal stuck its head up and from the pain and terror in her eyes, I could see that it was Mhairie. She barked in anguish, then ducked back into the ocean, searching.

Malcolm and I looked at each other for a second. "Come on," said Malcolm, "we have to get these people to hospital."

As we steered for Oban, we heard the roar of motors, and then a fleet of Sea Rescue boats powered into view. Most of the humans that were still alive had a good chance of making it.

People were everywhere on the floor of the Emergency Room, some being bagged and some being injected with roktopus antidote.

Junior doctors who looked scarcely older than Malcolm and me were shouting orders at each other and running around with drip tubes. TV crews had arrived and were running around with cables shouting questions and tripping up the junior doctors.

Malcolm and I split up and searched desperately along the rows of survivors, pushing away enthusiastic junior doctors who wanted to inject us, and begging the rescued: "Have you seen two women…red hair, black hair…very pretty?"

Those who still could move just shook their heads dumbly.

It was two hours since the monsters had spat out their poison. Our mothers weren't here, and if they were still in the water, they were gone.

I met Malcolm coming the opposite way down an aisle and we looked at each other wordlessly as reality began to sink in. We were both thinking about our moms, our dads, about all the motherless years ahead.

"*Ever, ever again*, Liam Padraig!"

Liam Padraig. L.P. Elpy.

It was Mhairie holding her wet, scared little brother by the hand, with Flims in the crook of her arm. She stopped dead and looked at us, her eyes deep with pain and sympathy, taking the situation in.

Her cell phone rang.

"Yes?"

After a minute, she held it out to me. "It's your mother," she said, "and she says she's watching us on TV."

Chapter Eight

Spikes In The Bahookie of
Damien Duke

So our mothers had caught the *ten o'clock* ferry.

By the time we fought the giant roktopi that destroyed The Viking Queen, they were already safe on Little Snugglay.

When Air-Sea Rescue began bringing survivors into the Oban Infirmary with their stories of the monsters and the beginnings of paralysis, the Chief Emergency Physician had called Malcolm's mother, the inventor of roktopus antidote and the only doctor with experience of using it in the field. She was already on her way back to Oban in a DODO 'copter.

Meantime, the island's population gathered around their visual display units to watch the online news.

As things turned out, Malcolm and I were not grounded, or even in trouble. Everybody was too relieved that we were safe, and my parents were annoyed with themselves for not taking my anxiety more seriously. They told Malcolm's mother that I was lucky to have him for a friend (no kidding).

Malcolm's mother was too busy and excited to be angry with anyone, anyway. They had machines in the infirmary that showed that the people rescued from the sea really did have signs of paralysis, and that her antidote really did work to reverse it.

No one had photographs of the roktopi, which had vanished before Air-Sea Rescue arrived. Also, after a night of sleep the survivors' memories of the events were hazy, and they were wondering themselves if it had all been a dream. No trace of roktopus toxin was found in anybody's blood.

The ferry disaster was put down to the storm, acknowledged to be one of the worst in Hebridean history. The paralysis and the roktopi stories were more difficult to explain. It was generally agreed that the survivors' nervous systems had been attacked by something that caused collective hallucination and temporary nerve block, and there were various theories: possibly a fungus growing in The Viking Queen's hot chocolate machine, or maybe an algal bloom in the ocean. Whatever, the paralysis had been real and Maggie MacDodd's antidote had cured it. It looked like she had invented a general facilitator of nerve function, which would have a thousand uses in medicine. Overnight, she became famous and was probably going to stay that way for the rest of her life.

The only person who caught a bad time was Elpy, which was fair enough in my opinion. Although it was sad to see his mournful little face in the window every time we went to Mhairie's house while he was banned from all outdoor activities for a few days.

I had to admit that my mom really did look like her old self again, and maybe even a bit better than that. Her face was smooth and rosy and her hair was shiny. My dad was still paying extra special attention to her, but not like he was worried, more like he couldn't believe his luck.

When I got home that day she was in the kitchen with my dad and a bunch of other theoretical physicists, clustered round the computer and arguing about sea monsters. There was a rumor going around that some had been spotted in our garden, as well as in the ocean, tearing the ferry apart. Nobody was taking this seriously, but they all had theories about what the rumors were built on. The melted window and the burn holes in the front door had been boarded up, and ikat patterned throw rugs were draped over the damaged sofas and armchairs.

Mom was chomping through a monster plate of Scottish breakfast, including baked beans, fried eggs, sausages, toast and jam and a big glass of milk.

My mom is really not a fried and dairy person, she is a bokchoy and carrot stick person, but I guess her body knew what it needed.

"Those must have been some primo vitamins," I said.

She swallowed and stopped munching for long enough to say, "But what I really want is Japanese noodle soup. You know, the udon bowls with bits of chicken and bokchoy and sea vegetables and slices of boiled egg."

"Good luck getting that in Wee Snugglay, I'm afraid," said Macallister, who had dropped in.

But this turned out to be yet another example of the art of the possible. There was a bunch of Japanese scientists on the islands and a whole posse of them drifted over that evening. Mhairie's mother's store now stocked a limitless supply of udon, and the Slumber Strait was a good source of wakame and other sea vegetables. Soon our refrigerator was chock with delicately carved and painted pots and bowls.

I was amazed that these people were so interested in my mother's food preferences. I guessed I hadn't been the only person to be worried about her.

"Mom, we're going to have to chuck some of this," I called, when I had to move six or seven refrigerated bowls to access the OJ.

"Over my dead body," she shouted back seriously, and then she and my dad dissolved in giggles like a couple of kindergartners.

I stuck a note on the fridge: *Museum of Noodles*. It was one more thing I would have to learn to live with.

"Frustrating," Macallister agreed, when I complained to him about it later. "But from what I've seen and heard recently, I'm now convinced that your mother's health is not a concern."

She was still a bit absent minded: like she put the honey in the oven and my socks in the dishwasher, but she had been like that before, so I saw no reason for alarm.

We had to postpone our raid on the main DODO compound because there was no way that Malcolm and I could sneak out at night with all the activity that was going on. The DODO was the center of activity, but there were still laptops running in remote locations, so the scientists buzzed around each others' houses for a couple of days like the entire island was an experiment. Which I guess it was. This was OK because it gave us a chance to rest up and be in peak condition. Macallister and Malcolm were making progress with their virus, but there were still a lot of kinks and we had to be really careful. It would be bad to go with something that might shut down irrigation programs in Africa, or start a nuclear war.

When we did set out to swap the programs it was on a night when most of the DODO staff had moved to Little Snugglay, leaving only a skeleton staff at the Great Snugglay compound, which suited us fine. Malcolm had sneaked out through his bedroom window. My parents were pulling an all-nighter at the Little Snugglay DODO. Now that my mom was better, they had relaxed and were comfortable leaving me on my own with a cell phone and instructions to call if I was worried. As if…

Having Mac next door also had a lot to do with this.

Mhairie, of course, did not need to sneak. All the Selkies knew what she was doing. Her boat was in amazingly good condition, considering what it had been through during the fight for the ferry. We crossed the strait easily at midnight. The stars were out, no moon, and the night was warm and still.

We tied the boat at a small docking station on the bigger island.

"Wheep!" said Flims.

"Shh, Flims!"

"Wheep!"

A delicate, tangy sweet scent drifted by. Thornego pods were rupturing.

"Guys, eat some of these! We need them!" I said.

Mhairie already had a handful, which was reassuring, and Flims dug into a pile of spilled seeds with both paws.

Malcolm, with the reluctance of people who know too much about too many things, eyed them suspiciously.

"Get over yourself already," I said.

"I prefer to wait until they've been tested on a few thousand healthy *human* volunteers."

"Just eat them," Mhairie said.

Obediently, he screwed up his face and slammed a palmful into his mouth.

I watched with interest as his expression changed. Surprise was mixed in with a growing calmness, and something else. Determination. His chest didn't exactly puff out, but it did seem like he got a little bigger.

"That's gallous!" he whispered. ("Gallous" is Scottish for "good").

Mhairie rolled her eyes.

Fortified, we set off for the main DODO building, staying under cover of the occasional, luxuriant trees.

"We'll slide in the back way," Malcolm said. "The front entrance has a desk and security guards, but there's a back door for deliveries and taking out the trash. I know the code to get in."

"Cameras?"

"I was thinking Flims could jump on the camera and cover the eye while you and I slip inside. Then Flims could wait with Mhairie and do it again when we're leaving."

"Can you do that, Flims? It's important."

"Wheep!" she could do that.

Mhairie wasn't happy about being left outside, but could see that the plan made sense.

"I know the locations of all the cameras inside and the times when the guards do rounds. We'll have thirty minutes to get in, change the programs, and slip back out again."

A sound like "Yuck! Yuck! Yuck!" drifted over a rise. This was the laughter of Damien Duke, who appeared with his cronies, The Thuglies.

"Freeze!" I hissed, but they had seen us already.

"Hey Anxious, did you lose your island?"

"Just minding our own business."

"And what might that be?"

I remembered that Duke's family lived on Great Snugglay. They had seen us on the Internet News, and some people were calling us heroes. This could not have been thrilling to Damien Duke. Worse, from the looks of things, they had been partying while their parents were gone at the all-nighter, and from the smell of things, they had got themselves some alcohol. This was bad.

I could feel Malcolm gripping his pointer and Mhairie tensing up. The Blackflash was no use against these monsters, so I only had my fists.

"Hey, Miss Caledonia! Do you wish to partake of the King of American beers?" Damien waved an open Budweiser. The others had bottles as well. This was really bad.

Mhairie stuck her nose in the air.

"Don't react," I muttered. "And Mhairie, if they jump us, get back in the water."

"As if," she hissed back.

"Don't provoke them. If we can't get rid of them, we'll have to abandon the plan."

The lights of the DODO were in sight. If we headed there, the guards would stop any fighting. Of course, they'd also see that we got safely home without disabling DODO/ DREAMON/17. But at least we'd be alive. At this moment, that seemed like the best course of action.

But I had not reckoned on the effect of Malcolm's first experience with thornego seeds.

"Hey, Damien Doo Doo. Been practicing some ancient caveman ritual?" he yelled, very un-Malcolm like.

"*What* did you say, Haggis Brain?"

"You heard me, Potato Face!"

He stood there, threatening with his pointer, and it occurred to me that he could do some very real damage with it.

Damien and the Thuglies put their heads down and ran at us like rams.

At the same time, the stars flickered out, the warm air turned chill and threatening, and that same old vicious wind began to howl. The night was lit by an eerie green glow that seemed to come from the air itself.

"Hello, Harry," I muttered. "So much for the foolproof plan."

We dealt with the oncoming muscle dudes easily. They were drunk, we were not, and they were running with their heads down.

Before they rammed into us, we stepped out of their way.

Thugly One ran into a tree.

"Nnnnh!" his arms wrapped the oak and it was like he was trying to kiss it. His face slid down its bark until he thumped on his knees.

Thugly Two got his feet tangled up in some creepers and landed stretched out flat in the long grass.

Damien Duke, the Dude himself, thundered past me into a stand of unripe thornegos.

"Aiya! Aiya!"

As he thundered through the stand, the sharp spikes on the bright pink pods poked through his jeans. He went down on hands and knees then lifted his hands, looking in horror at his palms, covered with thornego pods that were anchored to his flesh by their thorns. He started swiping them against each other, trying to shake them off, which made them break.

Unripe thornego seeds are green and slippery with an irritating mucus coating that causes an itchy white, bubbly rash. According to Mhairie, you can brew them into a tea that cures fish mites, but that was of no help to old Damien now.

In the weird light we saw the white spots rise up on the reddened skin of his exposed arms and face.

He managed to shake the pods off his swollen, bleeding hands, and shuffle backwards away from the plants.

I saw all of this out of the corners of my eyes. The fronts of my eyes were focused on something that concerned me a lot more.

Just at the edge of view in the shadow of a grove of mangroids lurked a blurry figure. I sensed, rather than saw, its evil smile. Harry! He swept his arms up. Oh boy.

The ground in front of us trembled and began to swell. Three mounds pushed up.

"Earthquake!" Malcolm yelled.

But it was not an earthquake. It was worse than that. The mounds rose quickly and then burst at the top, scattering clods of earth and grass as three enormous thornego plants broke out of the ground. Each was fifteen feet high and carried four to five pods—spheres the size of ten gallon garbage sacks, not quite filled with air, and covered with wicked looking six-inch spikes. They were bright pink and unripe—the dangerous kind.

The shadowy figure pushed at the air and a bunch of the thornego pods lifted off their branches and began drifting and tumbling through the air. At first, their motion seemed aimless and erratic. Then Damien, looking up from his bubbling palms, saw the giant spiky magenta balloons, enormous versions of the pods that had just spiked and poisoned him. He shrieked and stumbled backwards, trying to get away.

"I think they're attracted to movement!" shouted Malcolm.

"Or sound!" Mhairie hissed.

Damien turned around and ran. The airborne pods stopped drifting, paused for a second then all took off after him. The first pod caught up to him, and with an extra swoop it targeted his rear end, burying its spikes in his big squashy butt.

"Oof!" said Malcolm.

"Aiyaah!" yelled Damien, and went down on his hands and knees, gibbering in pain and terror.

The Thugly who had been hugging the tree, roused by the commotion, hauled himself up and began to stagger away. The pods that were not attached to Damien changed course and followed him.

The guards on duty in the DODO—their Pinochle game disturbed by screams that could no longer be explained as "kids letting off steam"—ran out with their AK-47s, leaving the doors open.

They stopped in the weird green light that made the clearing look like an ocean filled with giant floating puffer fish, trying to take it in. Some pods had already changed course, and were cruising towards them.

"Holy fricoli!" one gasped, and lifted his gun.

"Don't shoot the kids! Don't shoot the kids!" shouted the other, who was older and I guess had a stronger grip on himself.

But the first guard was completely freaked out and pumped a hail of bullets. Two of the thornego pods exploded in a shower of fragmented spikes and slimy, poisonous, green seeds that rained down on the Thugly who was stumbling away as well as the one who was still flat on his face. White blisters rose on their rapidly reddening skin and they added their screams to the general noise and confusion.

Meantime, under cover of the trees, Malcolm, Mhairie, and I edged towards the open doors of the DODO. A couple of pods followed us, but as we reached the DODO, I turned and zapped one of them into non-existence with the Blackflash, while Malcolm ripped the other one up with his trusty steel pointer. It popped like a balloon. The seeds sludged in a pile while the spiky skin drifted down and draped over them. Malcolm yelled in triumph at destroying an agent of Dwam entirely by himself.

We slipped into the DODO and I felt, rather than heard, Harry give a hiss of frustration as the door slammed shut. A third pod slammed into the closed door and ruptured, leaving a sticky mess of seeds sliding down the glass. Through it we saw the three Thuglies looking like weird, gabbling, pustular monsters, and the guards, who had made short work of the remaining pods, trying to help without getting poisoned themselves.

"They'll recover," said Malcolm. "This place is going to be crawling with army medics in thirty minutes. We should have time to get done and be out of here before they start checking inside." He sounded very confident and even like he was enjoying himself a bit, which might have had something to do with his thornego snack. I was feeling alright myself.

"Wheep!" said Flims, sticking her head out from my shirt for the first time since the attack and sounding very brave.

"That worked out well for us," Malcolm went on as we followed his lead to the locked room that housed the main computer. "We don't have to worry about cameras because the network's been disabled by Dwam energy. When they come back on, Flims can block them and they'll put it down to a scabby connection. Harry thought he was being smart. Those pods can't drain too much Dwam energy, but that rash could have put us out of commission for days—long enough for him to stage his final breakthrough while we were still swimming in calamine lotion."

"Not that smart," Mhairie pointed out. "Not smart enough to realize that Damien isn't one of us."

"Right," said Malcolm. "He served the human race today as a decoy."

We all laughed, grimly.

"Here we are," Malcolm said. He used his dad's codes to open the door and we entered the large, windowless room that was lined with banks of computer equipment. It was silent and sleeping.

"Right," said Malcolm. "Flims, jump up there." He pointed to the eye of a camera that was trained on the main console. Wheeping excitedly at her importance, Flims clambered up the computerized wall and settled herself on the camera, draping her paws over the eye. "Wheep," she giggled again.

"We'll have to wait till it comes on," Malcolm said. "There we go!"

A red light seeped around Flims' paws, a low electrical hum filled the air and lights on the computer banks began to blink as the network came back online.

"It's over outside," I said. "The guards will be calling for backup."

"Right. We've got maybe fifteen minutes. I know what I'm doing." He did. His fingers were flashing over the keyboards.

"What the two of you can do is locate the stored drives with DREAMON/17," he said. "Over there."

Mhairie was already checking the cubbies where the drives were stored alphabetically and by number. "Got them!"

After that, there was nothing for us to do but wait and watch as Malcolm pulled up lines and lines of code, and switched them for other lines and lines of code.

"Yes!" he said every so often, which meant that things were going well.

Mhairie showed me her watch. Twelve minutes had passed. We looked at each other and winced. We didn't want to interrupt him. Thirteen minutes. Fourteen.

"Malcolm," I said.

"Nearly there, nearly there!" More flashing fingers, more lines of code.

Sixteen minutes.

"Last step now."

Seventeen minutes.

"We have to get out of here!"

"Done!" The words *Operation Complete* flashed on the screen.

"Shutting down," said Malcolm.

Eighteen minutes.

"OK! Return the drives."

Mhairie grabbed the drives and slotted them back in their places.

The computer screen was black, with just the low hum and the maintenance lights flickering.

Twenty minutes. Flims was still draped over the camera.

"How we'll do it," Malcolm said, "is the three of us will get out the door and hold it a wee bit open. Then Flims can jump down, slip through, and we close it. The camera won't record anything.

"OK Flims?"

"Wheep!" she nodded from her perch on the camera.

So we did it that way. Flims was great. She waited until the three of us were outside standing in the corridor, with the door about ten inches ajar. We heard the soft thud as she leapt down, and then the soft scrape of her scamper across the floor. Her little lavender head appeared in the crack and she jumped joyfully into my arms, wheeping softly with excitement and pride. Gently, Malcolm let the door swing shut.

The building was silent.

"Did it!" Malcolm said. "We'll slip out the back like we planned. The cameras are on now, but I know where they are. Here's how we'll do it: When we get close to a camera that we can't avoid, Flims can get behind it and cover the eye from the back, like she did in the mainframe room. Then the three of us slip past it, and Flims jumps down. Anyone watching will just see a gap in coverage of a second or two and not think anything of it."

So that was what we did. Three times there were cameras that would have seen us, but they each had a tiny blind spot that Flims was able to use to scamper behind them, leap up, and cover the eye with her paws. Five corridors and two staircases later, the back door was in sight.

"Made it!" We were nearly there.

"OK, for this one, the camera's outside, trained on the door" Malcolm said. So, a little more difficult."

Mhairie and I groaned. "How can we open the door without being taped?"

"We can't. The only way is to disable the camera from inside." He paused, dramatically.

Mhairie sighed, "And your plan?"

"Actually, it's easy. I can do it by tripping the fuse."

The fuse box was on the wall next to the door, and Malcolm, who had all his bases covered, grinned as he produced the key.

"Alright, so you're brilliant!" Mhairie told him. "Will you please get on with it?"

"Since you ask so nicely." He tripped the fuse. We were clear. Malcolm held the door open for Mhairie, "After *you*."

"Don't push it," she stuck her nose in the air and walked through.

"Hey!" yelled a voice from behind us. "Just where do you think you're going?"

We froze for a few seconds then turned around slowly, raising our hands. Flims stayed sensibly hidden inside my shirt. The two guards were standing there. One was tall and skinny and looked about sixteen and very scared. He had some bumps on his face, but they were not a thornego reaction, just regular acne. The other was shorter, thickset, older and dependable looking, but he, too, was visibly shaken by what had just happened outside. In other words, they were both jumpy. They were also holding AK-47s, which are major firearms. The AK-47s were pointing at us.

Chapter Nine

The Terror In The Tails

Nobody spoke for a minute. Then…

"That's Rory MacDodd's boy!" said the pustular guard.

"What gives, Malcolm?" asked his companion.

Finally, they lowered their guns.

"Jings, you're a sight for sore eyes!" Malcolm said. He was still thinking fast, which was lucky, because I just stood there, opening and closing my mouth like a guilty fish.

Mhairie was thinking fast, too. "Those teenager thugs were chasing us," she said.

"You know Damien Duke and his pals?" Malcolm went on. "They were after Mhairie. We ran in here for protection."

"They'd been drinking," Mhairie continued. "Did they give you any grief?"

The guards looked at each other uneasily. "Not exactly," said the older guard.

"They won't be giving anyone grief for a while," Pustules agreed.

"So, what was the shooting?" I got involved, finally.

"Yeah," Malcolm said. "When we heard it we panicked and ran. There was no one at the desk."

The guards looked at each other again, even more uneasily this time.

"We hid out in a dark room and when it was quiet we decided to sneak out the back," Mhairie said.

"We couldn't call for help because our cell phones wouldn't work," I added.

"Right, right," said the guards.

"So you saw Damien and the Thuglies? Where are they now?" Mhairie asked.

"Paramedics took 'em to the infirmary."

"You *shot* them?"

"Naw, naw! Some kind of allergic reaction. Like I said, they won't be bothering you guys again."

"So who was shooting, and what at?" Mhairie pushed on, innocently.

They looked at each other again.

The three of us were silent, giving it time to sink in deeply that they: (a) had left a top secret defense facility unguarded in a foreign country, (b) had machine-gunned a bunch of overinflated seed pods, and (c) would be much better off if nobody knew that we had been here and what we had seen and heard.

By this time the Dwam denizen thornegos must have vanished, and the guards were likely doubting that the freaky events outside had even happened. I felt quite sorry for them.

"Don't worry about it," said Pustules suddenly. "Classified training exercise."

His colleague looked at him with surprise and new respect. "Right, right," he agreed. "Classified."

Then Pustules, with new confidence, said, "When you guys were out there, did you uh, see anything uh, strange?"

"Apart from Damien?"

"Like uh," he shrugged, "with the plants?"

The three of us looked at each other and shrugged.

"There are some weird plants here," I agreed.

"Yeah, right," Pustules said. "They chase you in here?"

"*Chase* us?" We looked at him like he was crazy. "No, Damien chased us."

"Right," said Pustules. "But did you see…?"

His partner cut him off. "Like we said, a lot of classified activity tonight. You kids best forget whatever you thought you saw here."

Then Malcolm said, "It's a lot to ask, guys, but we'd just as soon our parents didn't know we were over here at all."

The guards looked at each other, with relieved expressions.

"Not supposed to be out on the water after dark," I supplied, helpfully.

"That right?" said the older guard.

"See, we're in trouble as it is," I went on.

"A wee matter of sailing our boat in a storm," Malcolm added.

"Sure, we heard about *that*," Pustules became enthusiastic. "Saw you on the Netnews. You guys are heroes!"

"Naw," we all shrugged and looked embarrassed.

"Sure you are!" said Old Guy.

"Heroes or not, we're officially grounded," I said.

"Had to climb out a window tonight," Malcolm confided.

"Aw," Old Guy grinned. "Heroes are always misunderstood. We climbed out plenty of windows in our time."

"I'd like to hear about that some time," I said, "but right now we'd best climb back in those windows."

"Right, right," Pustules said. "Stay in the light and head straight home."

"And we won't say nothin' if you won't say nothin'," winked the other guard.

After a bit more arm punching and winking we finally said goodbye and headed back to our boat. Looking back we saw Pustules standing on a chair, while Old Guy gave instructions, trying to get the camera down so they could destroy the incriminating film.

We did go straight home, crossed Slumber Strait to Little Snugglay and trudged up the track to the village of Nap. Nothing else bad happened that night. Mhairie and Malcolm walked me to my door and we agreed to meet at Macallister's house the next morning for a conference. Then they went back to their own houses.

As I mentioned already, my parents were pulling an all-nighter at the DODO. They had left me a note and a cold pizza. I was exhausted, but too strung out to go to bed right away, so I sat on my bed with Flims and Dad 1's diary. Flims snuggled up to me making soft wheeping noises. She was used to me being sad when I read this book.

"OK, OK, Flims," I opened it at random.

My son, I read, *will be everything I'm glad I am and everything I wish that I could be...*

Ouch. He'd written that a month before I was born. I flipped the page.

Attacked by a horde of monster rokroaches today. Zapped them with five pulses each. Four not enough, six is overkill. Remember this for energy conservation in future encounters.

I made a mental note to self to use just enough Blackflash and not more.

Macallister says Murky Harry's getting stronger and he'll make his move soon. Can't be soon enough for me. I want this thing with the Dwam Dimension over. I need to get home. I miss Arla so much. A letter from her came on the boat from Oban. She says the baby kicks like a horse! We're calling him Angus and I feel like I know him already.

I closed my eyes, but felt tears squeezing through. Flims' soft little paws patted my face.

"Wheep, wheep," she said quietly.

"It's OK Flims," I said, and stroked her head. We fell asleep together, with the diary open on my chest…

My sleep was short but good. I cooked myself a decent breakfast because I figured I'd need it. I was scarfing it down, while Flims sat on the table eating magnolia petals, when my parents skipped in, flushed and giggling like excited little kids.

"Major, major breakthrough Angus," my dad said. "We may have definitive data by the end of the week."

Definitive data did not sound good to me.

"Don't overdo it," I said.

"I'm *starving*," said my mom. She picked a rasher of bacon off my plate and dangled it into her mouth.

"Hey! Make your own!" I protected my scramblies.

"I'll make scratch pancakes," my dad started cracking eggs. "And I'll bring you some in bed. Angus is right, Jools— consider your condition."

"What condition?" my antennae pricked right up.

"Oh, you know, that vitamin thing. Although I haven't felt this good in *years*."

But she did take the advice, and off she went to bed with *Chaos Theory Monthly*, half a cherry cheesecake, and a large bowl of cold Noodle Surprise with egg and bokchoy.

"Seriously, Angus, we're *this* close." My dad's thumb and index finger were a hairsbreadth apart.

"Excellent," I muttered under my breath.

"Angus, I hope you're OK with this—" he sounded concerned, "us working so much. It's not going to be for very much longer."

"Don't worry about me," I said. "I have plenty to occupy myself."

"Douglas Duke's son got himself in trouble last night," my dad said, sounding more worried. "Hospitalized at this point. Some crazy story about terror vegetation. Alcohol was involved, for sure, and I'm wondering what other substances. You're not involved in anything of that kind, are you Anxious? I mean, Angus? Some of the plant life on these islands may have hallucinogenic properties. That kind of stuff may seem cool to your age group, but it could do long-term damage."

"Seriously, Dad, I'm the last person to take any chances with the flora or fauna of this island."

And I left him to his griddle and his dreams.

At Macallister's house he and Malcolm were working on side-by-side laptops, heads bent together, making occasional exclamations of excitement or frustration.

"How goes it guys?"

"Getting close," Macallister said.

"Lucky break," Malcolm told me, not taking his eyes from the screen. "We hacked their emails. They're planning a definitive experiment."

"I heard about that. And it's a lucky break because?"

"The Definitive Experiment is to connect all their laptops in sequence and run DODO/DREAMON/17 on them simultaneously. This means that once we have our email virus, if just one advanced theoretical physicist opens his or her email when the laptops are connected the virus will spread and delete the program from all of them."

"Right," agreed Macallister. "So long as we have a virus before they run their test, we really can't fail."

"Of course, we'll still have Harry to deal with," Mhairie pointed out.

"Right," agreed Macallister. "There will be one last major battle. For that, Angus and the Blackflash are key. But without the energy from the program, I can't see Harry lasting too long. We're going to win this."

And he and Malcolm gave their full attention back to their VDUs. They were completely in sync. I envied them their focus.

Mhairie was rootling in the refrigerator, and pulled out the remains of a finnan haddie, which I had learned is a complicated seafood soup, and an acquired taste if ever there was one. Flims scampered over the table to investigate it, sniffed delicately, squeaked once and retired to a safe distance, perched on my shoulder. Flims loved fish soup, so this one must have had unexpected components.

"My mum makes this soup," Mhairie said, between mouthsfull.

Macallister said nothing, but had obviously heard her.

She slurped up a few more spoonfuls with a questioning expression.

"My mum *did* make this soup." She was looking straight at the back of his head.

After a minute, he agreed, "Aye, she brought it over yesterday."

She digested the information along with the fish.

"I can tell from the cilantro," she informed him.

"Mhairie, please stop talking," Malcolm said. "Make me a sandwich if you want something to do."

Her mouth opened and some small, transparent bones fell out.

"Come on, Varr," I said, quickly. "Not much for us to do here. I could use some help to practice."

I expected a meltdown, but for once, she did the sensible thing. She made a mean face at Malcolm's back but said nothing, except "Come on, Flims," and the three of us walked out into the golden morning.

We went down to the walled garden at the back of my house, which was a good, secluded place for Blackflash practice. We sat on a low stone bench in front of the chillypad-covered pond, contemplating the ruins of the gazebo that the acid poop-shooting caterpillars had destroyed. Frokhoppers croaked on the ice-crystal-covered chillypads and once in a while their long, sticky tongues furled out to grab a dragonfly. Frokhoppers, as I imagine you guessed already, are basically frogs that are covered in little green rocks. This popular adaptation occurred in at least four different phyla that I knew about now—not just species, but *phyla*. That amount of convergent evolution just doesn't make biological sense, and I had begun to wonder whether the Dwam Dimension was affecting reality here.

Birds were tweetling in the trees and a few baby scorpohamsters scampered around, grubbing for worms and fallen berries. Their bodies were about two inches long, soft and golden-furred, and their eyes were blue. They carried their poisonous stinging tails tightly rolled on their backs. I knew from my reading that these were a few weeks old—the tails, which had been white at birth, were beginning to darken. We both knew to be careful around them. Scorpohamsters are not usually aggressive, but if you step on a baby it will sting you—and at that age they can't control the amount of venom they inject so it won't be just a warning, it could be fatal.

"There must be a burrow under those bushes," Mhairie said. "Their parents will be close by, watching."

She was silent for a while after that. I wondered what was on her mind.

"What phylum is that anyway?" I said.

"Huh?"

"Scorpohamsters. They're half arthropod and half mammal."

She shrugged, like, *so what*? "Too bad they forgot to ask your permission to exist," she said.

"Do you think the Dwam Dimension influences reality?"

"Meaning what, exactly?"

"Meaning that these creatures are a biological impossibility."

She shrugged again. "*I'm* a biological impossibility."

"*Exactly.*"

She glared at me. "You think *I'm* a product of Murky Harry?"

"No, not a product..." I said quickly.

"A *by*-product?"

I stopped trying to explain, regretting I'd said anything. "Sorry," I said.

"Whatever."

It was the second time that morning that she had not taken a golden opportunity for a full on huff.

We were silent for a while, watching the scorpos.

"Do you think about your first dad much?" she suddenly asked.

"I was reading his diary last night. It was like he was speaking directly to me. Like he knew he wouldn't be around. Which I guess he figured was a strong possibility."

"I don't have anything like that from my dad," she said.

I said nothing, not knowing what to say.

But I have a good mom," she continued.

I realized she was working through some question out loud, so I kept my mouth shut.

"Macallister might make a good dad," she observed.

"The best," I agreed.

"Right," she said, like something was settled. "That was good, Angus. I'm glad we talked."

"We did?"

The wind changed, and the light did too.

Flims dived inside my shirt and shivered there. A mommy and daddy scorpohamster rustled out from under some bushes, squeaking anxiously, and rounded up the babies, herding them under the foliage to where presumably the nest was.

The frokhoppers stopped croaking and catching flies and flattened themselves out on the chillypads, pretending to be hills of green beans.

"Please, not now," I said.

Mhairie and I stood back to back, me looking over the pond to the ruined gazebo, she watching the dense, dark hedge of rhododendron bushes at the back of the garden. I held my Blackflash ready.

Nothing happened for several minutes, except that more and more color bled out of the day. The air felt cold, damp and nasty, and swirled in that circular wind I'd come to know and love so well. Leaves and feathers got caught up in it, sailing around and around.

"Stay calm," I heard Mhairie say, between clenched teeth.

"You talking to me or to you?" I tried a weak attempt at humor.

"You and me both, Anxious," she replied.

"He's trying to psyche us out," I suddenly said.

"Don't let him."

"He can keep this up all day if he wants to. Draining our energy while using almost none of his own."

"Don't give him ideas!" she hissed.

It was true, though. Macallister had said that one of Harry's tactics was to wear his opponents down with multiple low level attacks, while saving most of his power for his breakthrough battle. If he understood human psychology enough to figure out that he could sap our strength just with creepy sounds and visual effects, I might as well hang up my Blackflash right now.

For this reason, I was actually relieved when a couple minutes later, I heard a low, ugly hissing and saw a dark, man-size blur across the pond, wavering by one of the acid-scorched stone pillars of the gazebo, just out of Blackflash reach. The shape firmed up as though he was leeching substance out of reality—which I guess he was. His eyes glittered and his lips curled back, his mouth a blacker gash in the general murk of his face.

"We've got company, Mhairie," I said. We were still back-to-back.

"Bring. It. On," she answered, grimly. Mhairie is a seal you can count on in a crisis.

Harry lifted his shadow arms, summoning something.

"Oh boy," I muttered. I heard rustling from left and right, like elephants moving through brush.

"It's hamsters," Mhairie said.

"Hamsters with stingers?"

"Oh, aye. Angus, now would be a good time to turn around."

I hated to turn away from Harry, but really had no option. I turned my head quickly, to the right and then the left, and heard Harry cackle.

There were two of them, each the size of a jeep. Their golden fur looked soft and deep, their eyes were a heavenly blue, but mad and vicious. Two menacing, foot-long yellow teeth jutted over their lower lips and dripped with fetid saliva; their fat pink feet were tipped with four claws each the size and shape of meat hooks.

But the terror was in the tails.

The tails were green-black, crusted, and fifteen feet long. They were two feet in diameter at the base where they sprouted from the hamster butts, and tapered to glistening, wicked points that dripped sparkling globules of black poison.

Both wicked points were pointing at us.

If I Blackflashed one of them, the other one would get me.

"Over my dead body," murmured Mhairie.

"Not going to happen," I muttered back. I figured I might as well be skewered by two vile, poison-dripping furry animals as one, and in the process at least I could save her.

"Come and get me!" she yelled, and jumped at one of the hamsters.

"No, Mhairie!" I moved faster than I knew I could, grabbing her round the waist then threw her with all my strength over the low pond wall and into the pond. Her butt smacked onto the chillypads and she sat there for a second, her mouth an "O" of astonishment, before the skin of pads and thin ice gave way and she sank. The effort of throwing her pushed me down on my knees. There was a huge splash, indignant frokhoppers leaping and croaking, and I remember being hit in the face by a spray of little green rocks and water droplets.

The scorpos charged, one from the right and one from the left, the insanely sharp points of their venom-charged tails swaying in front of them. I was about to be double-kebabbed. I could see Harry grinning across the pond. Maybe not completely out of reach. I aimed the Flash and pushed the beam out with every ounce of hope and strength I had. He saw it coming, the wavy-air lancing for him straight and true, and his cackling stopped. He leaped up and backwards, his cloak flapping like a monstrous bat, and the beam passed harmlessly beneath him.

The scorpo tails lunged.

"Oof!" Something hit me in the stomach and my body's wind blew out of my mouth. The something carried me backwards through the air. My landing was fragrant and springy. Huge rhododendron flowers boinged around my head like purple footballs, while freezing dampness soaked my shirt. I had been thrown into the bushes by a large gray seal.

She had to have moved inhumanly fast. Which was not really surprising, considering that she is *not actually human*.

"Mhairie!" I gasped.

"Owp! Owp!" she shook water and icicles from her whiskers.

"Wheep!" Flims stuck her head out and nuzzled Mhairie's nose.

"The scorpos!" I wheezed.

We all jumped to look at once.

The scorpo tails, you will remember, had both lunged for Angus. But Angus had not been in their way. What had been in their way was the other scorpo. Unable to slow the momentum of their charge, each had skewered the other neatly, deeply, in the back of the neck.

"Squeeah! Squeeah!" they screamed, pattering around on their fat, naked feet, like two plush golden beanbags pinned together by two black, scaly, arching tubes of poison.

"Oh, gross!" I said.

They were unable to pull the tails out of the bodies, and with Harry vanished, were weakening rapidly. Eventually, they slumped sideways and lay there, huffing and shivering, like dying, yellow powder puffs. We watched until they were still, their borders blurred and they melted out of existence, and light and warmth leaked back into the day.

"Enough practice for today," I announced.

Then Mhairie slipped behind an ornamental fountain and reappeared as a person, dragging her skin behind her, and we headed back to Macallister's.

Our intrepid net-warriors were sitting at the kitchen table with the caterpillar tank between them, training the pillars to shoot acid poop at dandelions through a hoop. They jumped with concern when they saw us, so I guess I looked the worse for wear, because Mhairie looked fresh as a sea breeze.

"Don't ask," I stopped them. "Just tell."

They sat, though clearly still worried.

"We did it," Macallister said.

"You taught acid poop-shooting caterpillars to shoot acid through hoops?" asked Mhairie.

Malcolm smirked. "The virus is ready."

"You're serious?"

"Yup!" They began to relax again, and turned to the computer screens, demonstrating with lines of unintelligible script.

"The bottom line," Macallister said, "just as soon as one advanced theoretical physicist opens his or her email, DODO/ DREAMON/17 is history!"

When I got home, I felt almost sorry for my parents, who were tweetling like a pair of happy birds.

My dad was cooking squid in ink sauce and my mom was parading around in a blue velvet evening dress with small golden lobsters and other crustaceans embroidered on it. Her hair was in two long braids with dangling shells that clinked, and a glittering headband with reagle feathers stuck in the front.

"Yo, Angus," my dad said, "don't you think that's the perfect outfit for a Nobel Prize acceptance speech?"

Flims leapt onto the table and whooed in admiration.

"Yo, Flims!" said my dad. "I think so, too. Want some ink squid?"

He gave her a little dish with rubbery lumps floating in black soup, which she grabbed with both paws and started slurping contentedly.

"Maggie brought this back from London," my mom said, proudly, about her outfit.

"I didn't know she went."

"Presenting her data at the Royal Society," my dad said. "Maggie's work on the roktopus antidote is making her famous."

"I'm surprised *you're* not working." I looked around at dark visual display units and closed laptops.

"There will be time for that on Friday," (today was Wednesday). "Tonight, we celebrate!" my dad waved his spatula.

"And what do we do on Thursday?"

"On Thursday we get our ducks in a row," said my dad, "and on Friday we run the definitive experiment. Do you want your ink squid with rice or pasta?"

"Whatever," I said.

Do we have mashed turnips?" asked my mom.

"I'll have pasta," I said, quickly. "Back in five."

And I went in my room to call Malcolm. Things were working out. We had Wednesday night and all of Thursday for the advanced theoretical physicists to open their emails and destroy their copies of DODO/DREAMON/17 without ever knowing it.

My cell was dead.

A pit of dread opened in my stomach and I braced for another Dwam attack. Macallister had said that Harry might hit me with a lot of low-grade battles to wear down my stamina.

But the evening sun was beaming gently, and the air was sweet with cherry blossom and bird song.

"My cell's not working," I walked back into the living room. "Can I try yours?"

"No cell phones today," my dad said.

"How come?"

"We switched off the towers."

"What?"

"We want the best chance of picking up a really clear dreamon signal, if there is one," said my mom. "And we don't want any other coherent signals floating around. So we made a rule—no transmitting information from today until after the definitive experiment. The best way to make sure people follow it is to shut the WIFI towers down."

"Oh, man," I said. "I need to call Malcolm."

"Chill, Angus. You can run over to your friend's house if you need to talk."

"But people won't be able to open their emails!" I wailed.

"Angus, this is very important, and it's only for two days," said my dad. "The decision is made, the transmitters are down. Until The Definitive Experiment is done and dusted, there will be no cell phoning, no internet surfing, and *definitely* no opening up of emails!"

Chapter Ten

The Breakout Battle

There was no sign of Dwam for the rest of Wednesday and Thursday, as though Harry knew his chance to break through would come on Friday and he was resting up for it. We hung out at Macallister's house, figuring there was safety in numbers and keeping up our morale. I didn't practice, because it was better to save my strength.

Mhairie's mother, Sylvy, was there most of the time—she and Macallister having given up pretending that they were not a couple—along with all of Mhairie's curly black-haired Selkie brothers and sisters. Mhairie was happy to have them around because it meant that she did not have to worry. I have to say that Sylvy was a pretty calming influence. She behaved as if everything was normal and was talking about opening a seaweed fusion restaurant, all the while the kids were running around with buckets of wet flapping things or stirring pots that all seemed to be filled with stuff that was dark green and slippery.

Macallister said, "Mmm, *mmm!*" to everything he tasted but it tended to look a bit like this was because his lips were stuck together. I have to admit I was impressed that he had managed to have a romance at the same time as battling the dark side and creating an Internet virus.

The drylab at the DODO was a huge room with banks of computer equipment, telescopes, detectors for this and that, and a whole wall of colorful surfboards, parked there by their owners. The advanced theoretical physicists brought The Definitive Experiment laptops into this room on Thursday morning and there they sat, connected up in sequence in the drylab, all thirty-six of them. There were always at least six people with plaid shirts and beards, or parachute dresses and wind chime earrings fussing over the laptops, and Malcolm's dad, Rory MacDodd darted tirelessly between, adjusting here and reconnecting there, like a pediatrician in a special care baby unit. All of which meant that Malcolm had zero opportunity to grab a laptop and corrupt it. His dad refused to let him "help" and brushed him away absent-mindedly, which was pretty unusual. But most of the physicists had kids that they were vaguely aware were running wild while they hovered over their computers. And they were all going to make it up to us later.

What Malcolm did manage to do before they kicked him out, was slip a transmitter under my dad's desk so we would be able to hear what they were saying from outside.

On Thursday the islands were calm and sort of festive. It was sunny and warm, and kids were everywhere—boarding, blading, whatever, in greater numbers than usual. This was partly because of the ban on net surfing and partly, I suspected, because Damien Duke and the Thuglies were still in intensive care and not around to dominate the beaches. The teenage population was treating Malcolm and me with new respect—both on account of the story of The Viking Queen and also because of rumors that we were involved somehow in Damien's hospitalization. But we couldn't enjoy our new popularity, knowing what we knew. We mainly hung around Macallister's house and the Selkie network kept us informed of progress at the DODO.

Malcolm's and my parents were pulling all-nighters, including Malcolm's mom, Dr. Maggie MacDodd, who was in her biology lab, not wanting to miss the opportunity to analyze the Thuglies' pustular fluid while it was still fresh, and Malcolm's parents would not leave him in his house alone, so we stayed over at Macallister's. We all slept in the living room in sleeping bags, except for Elpy who preferred the kitchen sink. It was like camping out and was fun except that we knew we would have to battle Dwam next day. Macallister and Sylvy took turns telling scary stories with funny endings, and I fell asleep surprisingly early, grateful to be with friends.

On Friday, Macallister, Mhairie, Malcolm, Flims and I left at dawn after a breakfast of kippers, which I was beginning to get used to. Sylvy stayed at Macallister's with the younger Selkies, and before we left, a long look passed between her and Mhairie.

"Look after her," she told Macallister.

I would not have wanted to be Mac if anything happened to Mhairie.

We took up position under an oak tree, about 100 feet away from the drylab. Almost all of the adult Selkies from the islands were there, waiting in quiet groups. They had brought equipment, gathered from their day jobs as fishermen and coastguards. Under a grove of mangroids was a mound of bright orange rubber buoys, each about ten feet in diameter, like a pyramid of enormous oranges. Every so often, one would roll away and a couple of Selkies would have to run after it.

"What are they planning to do with those?" I asked.

"Och, whatever needs to be done," replied Macallister, cryptically.

They had steel wire trawling nets with small mesh—the kind that are illegal now because they trap baby fish. The Selkies didn't use them for fishing, but I could see that they would be useful against the denizens. And there were several huge harpoon guns, placed discreetly under trees. Probably also illegal, but kept in good working order for just this purpose—the battle with Dwam.

With binoculars and the transmitter we could clearly see and hear what was going on inside the lab. There were about twenty-four people in there, including my dad, my mom, who was sitting at a desk in front of one of the laptops with a sausage sandwich and a pint of chocolate chip ice cream, and Malcolm's dad, who looked like he was praying, which I guess he probably was. They were all vibrating with excitement. They had not had the sense to get a decent night's sleep and some of them were beginning to snap at each other. My dad was officially in charge, and I guess not all of them were happy about that, especially Damien Duke's dad. He was a burly advanced theoretical physicist, with straggly dark hair around a bald patch, a spiky black beard and a beer belly, who rolled his eyes impatiently every time my dad gave an instruction.

"Run it!" my dad's order cut through the tension, and my mom flipped a switch. All thirty-six of the laptop screens glowed green, then lines of 1s and 0s started running across them. There was dead silence. Then, "Detecting, detecting!" came my mom's clear voice.

We heard an ominous throbbing, first from the transmitter, then loud enough that we could hear it from the DODO itself. The whole building seemed to be pulsing.

"Contact! Contact!" yelled my mom.

The light changed. The temperature dropped at least thirty degrees. The sky was dark green and so low you could almost touch it. The circular wind screamed horribly, and the air itself was throbbing. Flims began to chatter in sheer terror and I clutched her through my shirt.

"This is the worst ever," said Macallister, grimly. The four of us pressed together in the gathering dark, as drops of freezing rain came down.

Impossibly, the six large windows of the DODO belled outwards, as though rubberized and were being blown into huge glass bubbles. Then the tension broke as they all smashed in unison and deadly shards of glass flew out from the building.

"Duck!" The fragments stopped just short of our stakeout place.

"Run!" I yelled. We pelted through the storm, our thick-soled sneakers crunching over the carpet of broken glass to the now empty windows of the drylab and began to climb over the sills.

"Angus!" yelled my parents together. "Watch the glass! Watch the glass!"

The drylab was complete chaos. The fierce wind outside was now inside. Papers and graphs caught in the cyclone, circled the room and scientists grabbed for them. A delicate Chinese lady was blown off her feet and smashed against a filing cabinet. Macallister dragged her under a desk and she lay there, stunned.

"Get Maggie MacDodd!" yelled my mom, who was gingerly dabbing an ugly scrape on a blond woman's temple. Maggie's lab, and a bunch of other medics, could be reached through a door at the back of the drylab, which some people were yanking on.

"We can't open the door!"

"Get the kids under the desks!"

"Watch the experiment!"

"What a time for a hurricane!" my dad yelled.

The computer tables were below the level of the windows and protected from the full force of the storm. The laptops were still running. I could feel the throbbing now. Shoom! Shoom! It vibrated through my bones in hungry waves. The rain was randomly coming down in sheets, lashing through the empty window, and hammering the floor. I looked down. An inch of murky water lapped around my hi-tops. A fleet of scummy bubbles swirled in.

In the frame of the empty window, deep black against the roiling green, I saw a man-size shape leer in for a second before it melted into the storm. Harry!

"Switch off the laptops!" I shouted.

Malcolm, Mhairie and I started pushing the power buttons, pulling cords out of the wall, and Flims, unusually brave, jumped onto the desks and scampered across them, ripping connections apart.

"Lay off The Definitive Experiment you twisted little freak!"

Something grabbed me round the waist and lifted me off the floor. It was Douglas Duke.

"Lay off my kid!" yelled my dad, balling his fists.

"My kid's lying in the infirmary looking like a black hole spat him out, MacDream!" snarled Douglas Duke. "And I think your freakoid little mutant had something to do with it!"

I was still dangling from his hairy arm. I realized how stupid and bad this all was. We were doing Harry's work for him.

"Dr. Duke! Dad! We have to switch off the laptops! The computers are causing the storm!"

"Brilliant deductive reasoning!" said Dr. Duke. "That'll get you places, kid. Jail, for instance!"

"Watch your tongue, Duke!" My dad lunged for him and twisted me out of his grip. I touched down behind my dad, and he and Duke faced off, circling each other like plaid-shirted bears. Freezing water soaked my socks. I looked down. Three inches.

"MacDream…" said Duke. His mouth dropped open before he finished his sentence, and the punch he had aimed at my dad's face dropped to his side.

The punch my dad aimed at Duke's face hit home. Duke's head jerked violently to the right but he stayed standing, slightly stunned, looking like—well, like he'd been punched in the face.

"MacDream…" he said again.

"Something to say?"

"Behind you…"

"Yeah, *right*…" said my dad.

"*Behind you Dad!*" I yelled.

My Dad's back was to the windows. He was about three feet in front of one of them, drenched and dripping from the pounding rain.

Over the sill snaked the tip of a green and purple, rock-encrusted tentacle, waving and probing for something to grab. Behind the tentacle, glowing faintly through the murk, the bulky head-body of a cephalopod, fifteen feet high, purple, green and knobbly, with two enormous eyes, protected like the eyes of the monsters that destroyed The Viking Queen by knobs of transparent quartz that glittered like the eyes of spiders.

Roktopus!

Fifteen feet of tentacle followed the tip through the window and wrapped twice around my dad, lifting him off the floor and shaking him like a terrier shaking a rat. Baseball sized green and purple rocks rained down. My dad's eyes were huge with surprise.

"Danny!" screamed my mom. She left the woman she'd been helping and tried to run to my dad, but two of her friends grabbed her and pushed her onto a chair. "Julia, stay!" they said urgently.

"Julia, stay!" croaked my dad. He was five feet off the ground. The monster began to swipe in wider arcs, and smashed him against a bank of computers.

"Put him down!" I screamed. I grabbed the Blackflash off my belt and aimed at the base of the tentacle. A long beam pushed out of the Blackflash, sucking my strength out with it. I severed the tentacle, which fell heavily, still squeezing my dad. He hit the floor, now five inches deep in noxious water, with a sickening thud. His lips were blue.

Douglas Duke pulled a six-foot telescope off its stand, and with a roar he ran at the beast and jammed the black metal cylinder into its rocky eye. The skin of eye-crystals shattered under the force of his assault, and then the entire head-body erupted in a geyser of bubbling black goo, which sprayed over Duke, dripping from his bald patch and his beard. He roared again, like a demented lumberjack, and twisted his weapon in the substance of the Dwam denizen. Tentacles whipped crazily as the thing endured its death throes; rocks flew, hitting several people hard and knocking a few of them out, and a fine black spray spat from its beaky maw into the eyes and mouth of its adversary, Douglas Duke.

Meantime, I dropped to my knees beside my dad, and sent a stream of rapid pulses into the ragged base of the tentacle that was still crushing his breath out. They traveled through it like balls of fluorescence, from base to tip and out again. Almost immediately, it loosened its grip on my dad, and as the wavy balls rocketed through, it began to jerk and crack like a snake with epilepsy. Finally, it split open like a hot sausage, spilling out chunks of shadow, which melted into the water on the floor until it was gone.

My dad sucked in a huge painful breath. "The heck is that thing?" he pointed, gasping, at the now twitching body of the roktopus. "The heck is *that* thing?" he pointed, wheezing, at the Blackflash.

"Don't talk, Dad. Try to get up." I was drained of energy myself, trying to push him up out of the filthy water. Then Malcolm was there helping me, and we dragged him onto a chair.

Duke, dripping black and sticky, was staring in bemusement at the creature he had killed. It was clearly dead, but not even beginning to disappear yet, which meant that it was nearly mortal. It was going to be harder for me to kill these denizens with the Blackflash, but easier for other people to help.

"I feel dizzy," Dr. Duke announced. Then he sat down hard. "Lipsh feel funny."

"He's going to need antidote," said Malcolm.

"They can't open the doors to let the medics in," I said.

My dad, still wheezing, demanded: "Julia, are we still collecting data?"

"Yes, honey, it's working." My mom still sounded OK.

The roktopus was at last becoming ragged around the edges. "What the...?" gasped my dad. He hobbled over to where Dr. Duke sat in the still rising flood. They both passed their hands through the now dissolving tentacles, blinking and shaking their heads. Duke's hands were beginning to tremble.

"See it's not a mortal creature, Dad. The experiment is causing this. We have to switch it off!"

But it was too late for switching off laptops—the ones we had switched off had all stayed on.

"It's a dreamon manifestation!" yelled my dad. "It's a new physical principle! Get it on film before it's gone!"

Malcolm and I left them trying to document their discovery amid the mayhem, and ran to the line of laptops and started banging them against the desks. After five or six bangs, two of them began to smoke and the lines of ones and zeros sputtered out.

"No!" Five or six scientists pulled us away. "This is the breakthrough of the century!"

There were thirty-four more laptops, still shooming excitedly. *Click, click, click, click, click!* Somehow I heard it over the noise of the storm and the screaming and shouting physicists. Over the six large windowsills scuttered twelve sets of livid green pincers, about the size and general deadliness of hedge clippers, and over the pincers wavered twelve sets of wobbling, green, googly eyes on stalks. Scrabs!

I pushed out a long beam and swiped it in an arc, aiming to cut the eyestalks—but in time they pulled their eyes down, close to their heads. They remembered. They dropped to the floor and sloshed through the water on their twelve skittery legs, claws clacking and slashing, fangs dripping venom, deadly black stingers carried just above the water line, ready to stab. The beam pulled my energy out with it and left nausea behind. I let it die and slumped, retching, against the wall.

"The stingers are poison!" Malcolm yelled. "Watch out for the stingers!"

A few of the physicists panicked, banging on the locked door at the back, or climbing onto computer tables, but I have to say that most of them rose to the occasion. Macallister and Malcolm's dad quickly formed a defense team with three other guys and three women. They grabbed surfboards from where they were parked against the wall and made a circle, facing outwards, swiping with the boards. It was very effective. The surfboards were long and heavy, the people were strong, and the scrabs, so close to mortality, were vulnerable to bashing. They were, of course, all female with a full load of babies, which clambered out of their bubbles and swam through the confusion, snapping and pinching where they could. Again and again the scientists thumped the arthropods, breaking legs and cracking carapaces. Meantime, others used nooses of computer cables to lasso the eyestalks and pull off the eyes. They came off with a squelching sound then bobbed nastily in the slimy soup. When the monsters were exhausted, clacking feebly but still dangerous, the team banged the surfboards on top of them and then jumped with both feet onto the boards. The shells shattered and body fluids spilled out with a sickening shlooping sound. The scrabs were dead, but did not disappear.

"I've been stung!" yelled one of the physicists, panicking slightly. "Only by a baby!"

"Me too!" yelled another.

Meantime, Douglas Duke was twitching on the floor and my dad was giving him mouth-to-mouth resuscitation.

"We need antidote! Where are the medics?"

I made to go and help, but stopped—"We've got this, Angus! Save it for Harry!" yelled Macallister.

I knew he was right and turned to the windows, scanning for my enemy. There he was, just out of range of the Blackflash, looking solid and hissing gleefully. He gestured to the horizon with a flourish then vanished, leaving his cackle in the air. I stared at a thick bank of green, rolling in fast from a distance.

"Fog?" I looked at Malcolm.

"That's not fog! It's the sea! Tsunami!" Malcolm yelled.

The wall of water rushed towards us, twenty-five feet high. There was nowhere to go. It whacked the building and hammered through the windows, carrying people with it and slamming them against the back wall. For a minute or so the drylab became a tank. That minute is definitely a contender for the position of Longest Minute of My Life, although it does have some stiff competition. The world was green and sound was muffled; the panic and confusion around me happened in slo-mo. People were flailing, trying to get out or to help their buddies, all of them exhausted and some badly hurt. The water was thick with scrab fragments and tasted disgusting.

I saw my mom struggling to get to a window, and cried out for her, but only bubbles came out of my mouth. I saw Malcolm making crazy hand signals, and Macallister supporting an unconscious woman. My dad had his hand under Douglas Duke's head and was trying to lift him. Meantime, Duke was seriously convulsing. Beyond help, I figured, and felt a pang of sympathy for Damien. His dad might be a thug, but he was brave. A sleek, muscular body thumped against me and I grabbed for the Blackflash, preparing to fight, but the creature nuzzled my face and huge black eyes looked into mine before it shot past and out of the window like a gray torpedo. Mhairie! Immediately my spirits lifted. Somehow we were going to get out of this.

The water receded, sloshing back out of the windows, leaving the drylab about two feet deep. There were gulping sounds as people sucked air, spluttered and hurled.

At the same time, the back doors opened. Mhairie had swum around to the other entrance and alerted the rest of the building (changing into a human at some point along the way). She appeared in the doorway, shaking her curls, with Maggie MacDodd, three other medics, and two guards with AK-47s.

"Help us! Help over here!" people cried. The guards and medics waded through the room, pulling out the injured and paralyzed. "We need to bag this guy!" they yelled over Douglas Duke, and I hoped he'd make it. My mom still looked OK, though a couple of medics were making a fuss of her, and my dad was gray with concern and remorse.

"My fault! My fault!" he muttered. "Should have lishened to Angus!"

"That'll be the day!" I muttered, under my breath.

"Shorry, Angush!" said my dad.

Shorry?

His legs started to waggle and his knees gave way. My dad needed antidote. Probably poisoned from giving mouth-to-mouth to Douglas Duke.

"My dad needs help!" I yelled.

"I've got it!" Maggie looked up from injecting Dr. Duke, who was being carried on a stretcher, and I figured I'd trust the medics to take care of it. At least this got my parents out of the way while I battled the forces of darkness. I hadn't seen Malcolm's dad for a while and hoped he was OK.

What I noticed next was that the deluge had accomplished what we could not. It had shut down all the computers. I thought it was lucky we had not been electrocuted, but then I remembered—salt water: the conductivity had protected us.

I remember thinking, *this is a break*. Not all of this is bad.

But a lot of it was still bad.

"This is his last chance, Angus!" Macallister yelled. "He'll throw everything he's got at us. Look out of the windows!"

I looked. I had been wondering why no Selkies had come to help us with the scrabs, and now I understood. I stood at the window with Macallister, the water above our knees, awestruck at the scene.

After the tsunami and under the still relentless rain, the ground outside—like the drylab—was under two feet of water.

From the West, where the ocean was, came the roktopi—about thirty of them, purple and green, some the size of smart cars and some the size of Mack trucks—scuttling on their tentacles like giant water spiders. "Hooo! Hooo!" they foghorned.

From the East, where our village sat, about twenty long green shapes rippled rapidly through the flood, push-pulling like monstrous inchworms. Gradually, they came into focus and, one-by-one, they reared up and identified themselves. Acid poop-shooting caterpillars!

Meanwhile, from directly in front of the drylab, a scurry of furry golden scorpohamsters, each ten feet long with fifteen feet of deadly tail, scampered on their fat, pink, taloned feet, their blue eyes blinking with menace.

The Selkies were fighting them off, some in seal form, others human. Selkies are taught from infancy that the smart thing to do in the Breakout Battle is not to kill the denizens, since dead ones would quickly be replaced, but whenever possible, to disable them so that they would drain their master's energy. This was why they had brought the steel nets.

The three nets were huge, the size of a football field. In seal form the Selkies dragged them with their teeth, ten on each side, swimming easily through the shallow flood until they reached the oncoming gaggle of roktopi. As the first Selkies came close, the roktopi grabbed for them, but their tentacles closed on emptiness as the leading seals launched themselves into the air, up, up and over the monsters, dragging the front edges of the nets with them. Then the pair of Selkies behind jumped, still with the net in their teeth, and then the pair behind them, each at the right time and in perfect formation, until the net was completely off the ground, stretched out and hovering for a second above the writhing denizens below it, with twenty Selkies dangling from its borders.

The Selkies dropped, and the nets dropped with them, falling neatly over the throng of hooing headbodies and seething tentacles. The seal people flashed through the water, pulling the edges of the nets together and tying them fast, making three enormous steel mesh bags, lumpy with furious cephalopods that were tangled together like parcels of parasitic worms.

A few tentacles separated before the nets closed and took off by themselves, naked white flesh glistening after their rocks were thrown, but most were trapped with the headbodies, grinding their rocks into green and purple powder on the steel wires of the mesh.

"That's good," Macallister said.

Meantime, other Selkies made inspired use of the orange rubber buoys. As the scorpohamsters came scampering viciously, their deadly spiked tails unfurled and dripping with venom, screaming, "Squeeah! Squeeah!" the seals swam to meet them two at a time, each pair pushing a buoy with their noses while a third balanced on top of the rolling orange ball. At the last minute when the scorpos stabbed, the Selkies jumped off the buoys and into the deluge, surfacing at a safe distance. The scorpohamster tails pierced the tough orange rubber of the buoys.

"Squeeah! Squeeah!" they screamed. In rage and frustration they waved their tails, thumping the buoys left and right like wicked pompoms on a bendy pole, their golden fur becoming wet and matted as the buoys splashed down again and again.

A couple of them swung their tails at the tails of other hamsters, banging the buoys against each other, trying to dislodge them. But they could not shake the buoys off.

"That's very good," said Macallister.

The Selkies who remained humanoid were riding the caterpillars. Holding hair spikes for balance, they stood directly behind the head segments, with a foot dug into the soft flesh where the head and the segment behind it were linked. By twisting this foot and pulling on the hairs, they controlled the direction of the grubs, which bucked and reared, trying to throw the Selkies off, the six little eyes on each side of their heads straining to see what was itching them, and black saliva spraying. But the seal people held fast and steered the giant larvae directly into the path of the remaining scorpohamsters.

The scorpos continued their pattering rush, their deadly spiked tails unfurled and dripping with venom, jabbing for the Selkies and squealing, "Squeeah! Squeeah!"

At the last minute, the Selkies jumped off the caterpillars and into the deluge, surfacing as seals at a safe distance. The scorpo tails pierced the tough green hides of the caterpillars. The larvae hissed in pain and fury and their bodies convulsed. The head ends spat ropes of liquid white silk, while the tail ends reared up and shot five-gallon acid poops.

The silk hosed more than fifty feet, to where the double file of rokchiks were chicken-stepping and wrapped them tight, hardening immediately, gluing their rocks to their feathers and their wings to their bodies, while their feet, under water level, stamped furiously. Unbalanced, they banged into each other and fell over, struggling and ackling in outrage, while the Selkies, apparently resistant to caterpillar silk, shot out of reach.

The acid poops flew even further, all the way to where the roktopi writhed in the steel nets like a nest of oversized vipers.

"Hooo! Hooo!" the mollusks bellowed as the acid poops scored direct hits on their bumpy, crystal eyes, which blackened and puckered as they melted.

Blinded and agonized, the creatures whipped in frenzy. A barrage of sparkling gemstones struck the water, like machine gun fire and more and more tentacles, ripped from head-bodies, went sidewinding through the soup to wrap and squeeze whatever other denizen they caught, adding to the mayhem.

Meantime, where the scorpo tails had stabbed the caterpillar skins, the wounds leaked a sticky black goo which hardened like cement—a survival feature, designed to close the wounds, which instead sealed the hamster tails firmly in the larval bodies. The scorpohamsters and the caterpillars were locked permanently together and began a crazy dance. By turns, the hamsters waved their tails and the caterpillars, lifted off the ground, snapped and waggled like rubber bands, spraying silk and acid poop over an even wider area, and then the larvae, set down again, twisted and jackknifed, thumping the hamsters right and left like vicious pompoms on a rope, their golden fur becoming wet and matted as they splashed down again and again.

Not all of the Selkies escaped without injury—their battles with Harry always took a heavy toll—but there was no question that they were holding their own.

Mhairie and Malcolm had been helping to get all the scientists out of the drylab. Now they waded over to stand with Macallister and I.

"The world sure owes those Selkies," I said.

"Aye," said Macallister. "And they'll never know it.

"Harry can't sustain this for long," he continued. "Those denizens are disabled, but still alive, draining his power. Now, Lad, we've our own battle to fight. Don't try to do it all. Go easy on yourself where you can—we need you to take care of Harry."

I looked where he was pointing. Several denizens had escaped the carnage, and were heading for the drylab. There were three roktopi, the bumpy purple and green head-bodies ten feet high, the tentacles thirty feet long, the multifaceted eyes the size of soup cauldrons, and two giant caterpillars, with nine hooked feet waggling on each long, spiky, segmented body, mean little eyes glittering, six on each side, and each face dominated by a rank, black, oozing, dripping maw.

"What now Mac?" I hoped Macallister had a plan.

"First, nothing," Macallister said.

"Come again?"

"Step back."

Macallister, Mhairie, Malcolm and I, with Flims peeking out from my shirt, waded backwards to the far wall. We were the last people left in the room.

"Grab a board!" said Macallister.

We each held a surfboard in front of us like a long shield. Mine was a Quicksilver painted with roses—it was Malcolm's dad's, I think.

The roktopi reached the building first. Their rocky, rubbery tentacles slithered through the windows, grabbed the frames and tore at them, pulling bricks and snapping joists like matchsticks. They were tearing the wall down. Their long tentacles snaked across the room, snatching and probing, but we were just out of reach. They hissed in frustration and continued to rip the building apart.

"Uh, you think we might want to do something Mac?" Malcolm said, nervously.

"Stand fast," said Macallister, between clenched teeth.

A green hairy caterpillar face filled one of the other window frames, and then another. Their mouths opened wide, black, spongy and wet, big enough to swallow a kid whole, with two rows of needle-sharp teeth that I had not noticed in our last encounter, dripping black, stringy, saliva. Their fetid breath cut through the rain and stung our eyes and nostrils.

"Ugh! Gross! See a dentist you slimy bags of poo!" yelled Malcolm.

"Brace for acid poop!" barked Macallister.

We stood firm behind our boards.

The green hairy faces dropped below the windows. We saw spiky green caterpillar butts lifted into position. Thwap! Splat! Acid poop slapped our boards and the wall behind us. The boards smoked and fizzled as their fiberglass reacted with the acrid chemical gunk.

Then again—Thwap! Splat!

A rash of small bubbles pocked the back of my Quicksilver.

"Not gonna hold, Mac!" I shouted.

"Stand fast!"

"Hooooo! Hoooo!" A siren scream of terror, rage and agony howled above the din. One of the roktopi had stopped junking bricks and was flailing erratically, whipping the giant grubs and its own fellows indiscriminately. One crystal eye was black and melting. Acid poop!

"The caterpillar bombed the roktopus!" Mhairie shouted.

Green and purple rocks flew in all directions, hammering our boards, thumping holes in the swollen caterpillar bodies, from which greenish black liquid spurted and then congealed. Crazed with pain, the injured roktopus wrapped a tentacle around a caterpillar and squeezed. Like a long balloon twisted in the middle, the larval monster inflated at both ends, the skin, bristling with hair spikes, stretched almost to transparency over the jumble of black tubing writhing inside.

"She's gonna blow!" yelled Malcolm.

With a horrible hissing squelch, the caterpillar exploded, from the head end and the butt end at the same time. Its stinking, corrosive body fluid sprayed in two wide arcs— some spattered the drylab, but most hosed the roktopi, all of which hooed and whipped their arms wildly. The air was dense with rocks, now coated with toxic black slime. The empty caterpillar skin, picked up by the whooping wind, dropped like a tent over a roktopus, which thrashed in blind circles, its tentacles hopelessly entangled in the empty green bag.

"MacDreeeam!" Somehow his evil hiss rose over the commotion. Harry! He was standing in the centre of the battle, just out of reach of the Blackflash. He raised his hands and dropped them in a chopping motion. Instantly, the two

roktopi that were still free, though maddened with pain, began to separate a tentacle each.

As the monsters twisted violently, one of the thirty-foot, rocky, sinuous whips spun off in an unintended direction and wound around the remaining caterpillar, squeezing its insides out like black toothpaste from a hairy green tube. But the other was thrown into the drylab, where it lashed blindly in the flood. We pressed against the wall, behind our boards, trying to stay out of reach.

Harry made the chopping motion again. Another two abominable arms snapped loose. Again, one spiraled away, while the other slapped into the drylab, probing and grabbing.

Harry chopped again.

I had no choice. I threw out a long beam. The headbody of one roktopus absorbed the Blackflash energy, swelled and vibrated. Its rocks crumbled into green and purple dust and the repulsive, slippery mass beneath fizzed and evaporated in a rain of shining sparks.

I retched. Macallister was holding me under me arms, otherwise I'd have slumped into the water.

There was still one roktopus left, and two tentacles in the water. Somehow, Mhairie had transformed into her seal self and was leaping between the tentacles, taunting them and causing them to wind around each other, while Malcolm poked them with his extensible pointer.

I leaned back against Mac, and with my remaining effort, pushed another longbeam out. The roktopus froze with a third tentacle hanging by a strip of skin, and finally disintegrated like the first.

Malcolm and Mhairie had managed to tie the two disembodied tentacles together around the legs of a steel table, where they coiled and slapped, but could not reach us.

I could hardly stand. But there was no time for resting.

"It's not over yet, Angus," said Macallister, grimly, "and only you can finish it."

I knew he meant Black Harry. I had one final battle to fight. I thought about my moms, I thought about my dads, and strength infused my limbs again.

"Take Flims!" I pushed her at Malcolm, sloshed through the grisly flood to the far window, which was unoccupied by dying monsters, and leaped over the sill.

"You want a piece of me?" I yelled into the wind, sounding a lot stronger than I felt.

"*Hssssh!*" The sound was pure evil. I followed it to higher ground, where the land was soggy but not under water. He pulled his substance out of the storm, condensing into an inky, man-size shape in a hooded cloak.

"*MacDreeeam!*" The word was thick with hatred.

I pulled my Blackflash and started to fire, rapid pulses into his chest. The effort depleted more of my energy. He was gone.

"*MacDreeeam!*" This time he was behind me. I whirled, and stumbled from dizziness, but stayed on my feet. His hands were filled with darkness, the size of a beach ball. *Darkball!* He threw. The thing flew at my head; it was thick and soft. I pushed out a blade, sliced upwards, and the thing pfutted out of existence in a shower of black sparks.

Harry threw again and I sliced the second one.

I tried to stay focused on what my dad had written about his battle with Harry, and what Macallister had told me: *Don't waste time on the edges. Go for the core.*

My dad had waited for Harry to tire and leave his midsection undefended, then put all of his strength into targeting his belly. So that was my game plan. *Wear him down. Then go for the core!*

It was easier said than done, however. Harry kept me off balance, chucking his black clods, wearing *me* down, staying always just out of Blackflash range. Then he tricked me into making a fatal mistake. As though overconfident, he danced towards me, closer and closer until he was within easy reach.

Forgetting my strategy, I threw out another long beam. He sidestepped it easily, cackling delightedly. I sank to my knees, nauseated and shaking. With a shock of real fear, I saw my beam die back to a tiny flicker of wavy air. With all my resolve I could not push it further.

I looked up at a darkball that was coming straight for me. I had no time to dodge, and my blade was only an inch or two long. Bracing, I shoved my hand and my weapon into the mass of shadow. It felt like freezing mud crawling with insects. It dissolved around me, leaving me breathless and nauseous.

Another darkball was coming. I rolled to the side, out of its path and the ball splashed on a mangroid, which instantly warped and twisted, its flat, rubbery leaves and magnificent white flowers thudded, heavy and rotten, on the swampy ground.

I struggled to my feet and swerved to avoid another inky comet, trailing shadows, that splatted on a boulder. Acrid smoke filled my nostrils as the stone began to melt and bubble like cheese burning on a grill.

I remembered the quote from Charles Darwin that my dad had written on the flyleaf of his diary: *The species that survives is not the strongest, nor the most intelligent; it is the one that is most adaptable to change.*

I was going to have to adapt to being without a Blackflash.

I had one chance left. I couldn't operate my weapon, but my arms and legs were still working.

This is for you, Dad! I muttered. Where I got the strength to do this is a mystery to me, but I pushed myself up and into the branches of a mangroid tree. Harry drew his black lips back from his black teeth and laughed his black laugh exultantly, gloating. Taking his time, he let his hands fill up with Dwam Substance—an enormous, flabby collection.

As he raised his arms and the darkball flew, I dived under its trajectory and it went over my head. I smelt scorched wood as it crashed the mangroid branches behind me, which curled inwards around it as the tree imploded in a downward, creaking rustle that ended in a singed squelch, and a charred and melted lump.

Holding the Blackflash in both my outstretched hands, pushing out a few, precious inches, I passed under Harry's hands and hit him in the stomach. My tiny blade stabbed through him and out the other side, and I followed it, leaping through his darkness, which slithered around me like a barrelful of black maggots. I landed in soft grass, shivering with shock and disgust, then forced myself up to face him again.

Only the edges of him were left, his head, arms and legs beginning to blur and quiver, his body replaced by an Angus-sized hole that he was staring down at uncomprehendingly. He looked at me and opened his mouth for some final curse, but it was lost in the wind as Harry thinned to shadow, and drifted away.

The sky cleared and lifted, as daytime leaked back into the world. The air smelled sweet and moist, and the flood dried quickly as I limped back to the DODO. Most of the denizens were gone already, others dissolving. One scorpohamster, its fur singed and sticky with acid poop and studded with gems, lay on its side, shuddering, its tail stinger buried deep in the headbody of a dying roktopus that gleamed white and defenseless, its rocks spent in battle. A couple of caterpillar skins flapped in the now gentle breeze like spiky groundsheets. The Selkies were gathering their dead and wounded. Again they had paid a terrible price in defense of reality.

What had been the drylab was a junkyard of twisted, smoking equipment and smashed furniture. The boards we had used for protection were warped, blackened lumps. My friends gathered around me, laughing and crying at the same time. *Wheep! Wheep!* Flims soft little arms crept round my neck. There were some small burns, but they would heal.

"So it's over, Mac?" I said, and in that moment felt a strong and thrilling connection to my father.

"Over, son," said Macallister, "and this time let it be for another hundred years."

But I was not so sure.

Epilogue

After the disaster of The Definitive Experiment, the DODO decided that the Snugglays were not the best place to conduct particle-wave-particle dream research—something about electromagnetic radiation disrupting computer networking. Everyone except Macallister, Malcolm, the Selkies and I had forgotten what had actually happened, and just remembered storm, flood and unexplained injuries.

The DODO buildings would stay on the islands. There were still many new species to discover, and a lot of them might have important uses in medicine and defense. Maggie MacDodd was leading the research effort. She was probably going to win a Nobel Prize before my parents, but only for physiology and medicine, which was not hard science, so did not really count. Not really.

My parents thought The Definitive Experiment had worked. They had enough lines of undecipherable code stored on their flash drives to excite them, and they were going to wow the "advanced theoretical world" when they figured them out. All copies of the program that could have read these codes had been destroyed, but they did not know this. Its name had been given to a completely different program, so they believed that they still had the original. The frustration and argument that this would cause kept them happy for months.

On the morning of the day we left, they were excited about the contents of a brown envelope with OBAN ROYAL INFIRMARY stamped on it. Some biophysicist collaborator, I figured. They were still clutching their envelope when we got on the little boat. On the dock, Malcolm stood between his parents, and Mhairie was with her mother, Macallister and all the little Selkies.

"Stay cool, guys!" I told them.

"Next summer, Chief!" Malcolm punched my arm.

"Stay Anxious, Angus!" Mhairie gave me a quick hug.

"Angus, you did your dad proud, said Macallister. And I knew he was right.

When the goodbyes were over and we were cleaving through the open ocean, Flims in the prow with her nose in the wind, my dad said, "Angus, we have something to tell you."

"Yeah?"

"Remember your mom was sick and went to the mainland for tests?"

"You said she was OK!" My alarm was instantaneous.

"I'm very OK, Angus. More than OK!"

"We were ninety percent sure back then," my dad waved the brown envelope from the Royal Infirmary. "Today we're completely sure. Normal boy!"

"Huh?"

"It's a boy!"

"You're—pregnant?"

They giggled, "The weird food choices should have clued you in."

"A brother?"

"You're pleased about this, right?"

I grinned, "Just don't call him Dreamon."

They looked at each other, guiltily.

"Oh, man!" I rolled my eyes. "This kid is so going to owe me."

My mom hugged me. "This is better than a Nobel Prize, right hon? Danny?"

"Our time will come."

"Maybe we should have gone into medicine."

I looked back and saw a flash, the wink of Macallister's telescope, trained on the boat. As I watched, the light distorted, became fragmented and elastic, as though some invisible force was manipulating it.

My stomach lurched with dread. Then, a gathering dark coalesced, drawing in and becoming denser, like substance trying to form. For a second, it blotted the light out completely then exploded silently in a shower of small black stars, before fog descended and hid the Snugglays from view.

Department of Defensive Operations (DODO)

Field Guide

The Wildlife and Plantlife of the Snugglay Islands

Department Of Defensive Operations (DODO) File
Wildlife of the Snugglay Islands
0001: *Scorpohamster*
Kingdom: *Animalia*; Phylum: *ArthroChorda*

Habitat

Scorpohamster is found only on the Hebridean islands of Great and Little Snugglay, off the West Coast of Scotland. There are two large colonies, one on the slopes of Ben Snore, the central hill of Great Snugglay, the other on Little Snugglay's Ben Slumber. The animals live in communal burrows beneath the long grass and heather, where they huddle for warmth and protection.

Characteristics

The soft, furry bodies of these shy, inoffensive creatures are well defended by the crusted, black, venomous tail. Adult scorpohamsters are typically 6 cm (4 inches) in length, while the tail can easily reach 15 cm (10 inches) fully extended. The tail is carried rolled in a tight coil, but scorpohamster can unroll and extend it rapidly, and can whip it with great speed and extreme accuracy in all directions, facilitating delivery of venom with deadly precision. Supplies of an antidote to the venom are maintained at the DODO clinic on Great Snugglay, and at the Oban Infirmary.

Diet

Scorpohamsters enjoy nuts and berries, supplemented by worms and grubs. They are particularly fond of the crunchy rokroaches that colonize the Snugglay beaches, and will leave the safety of their covered burrows in pursuit of this delicacy.

Behavior

Scorpohamsters are unaggressive, and have few enemies, save for the Snugglays' top predator, the reagle. One sting from the tail of an adult scorpohamster can easily kill a reagle, and encounters between the two species, though fortunately uncommon, are dramatic.

Babies are defenseless, with tails that are soft and white, and do not emerge from the burrows until the tail begins to darken and develop its crusty exterior shell. The adults huddle around the infants in groups until they are almost fully grown with acceptable tail control. During the months of July and August, adolescent scorpohamsters may be dangerous to humans, since they like to play in the long grass and can deliver a lethal sting if stepped on. Sturdy footwear is recommended.

Reproduction

Babies are born in April, emerge from the burrows in May and June, and are fully grown by September.

Status

Like all newly discovered species of the Snugglays, scorpohamster is protected, and removal of these creatures, or disruption of their habitat, is strictly forbidden.

Department Of Defensive Operations (DODO) File
Wildlife of the Snugglay Islands
0002: *Roktopus*
Kingdom: *Animalia*; Phylum: *Mollusca*

Habitat

Roktopus is found only in the Slumber Strait, the channel of water between the Hebridean Islands of Great and Little Snugglay, off the West Coast of Scotland.

Characteristics

These shy, intelligent cephalopods have a body, with a central mouth and a hard beak, and eight tentacles. They have large eyes and extract oxygen from the water with gills. Adult male and female roktopi are typically 4 inches in diameter, but may grow to the size of a soccer ball, with tentacles that can measure up to one metre (3 feet) long. There is no internal skeleton, but in health the animals are completely covered with small rocks. Sodium Carbonate and Calcium Chloride, secreted separately from ducts co-localized in the skin, react to form the Calcium Carbonate "rocks" which remain anchored to the ducts:

$$Na_2CO_3 + CaCL_2 = 2NaCl + CaCO_3$$

The rocks are uniformly spherical. Roktopus can control their size to some degree by controlling the rate of secretion, but they do not exceed 1 cm (.5 inch) in diameter.

The calcium carbonate, which forms the rocks, is naturally white, but roktopus can add pigment to the ducts, providing the opportunity for camouflage. The classic purple and green colouration of wild roktopi allow them to blend easily with the bed of the Slumber Strait, which is rich in amethyst and chalcedony. Roktopi studied in captivity alter their colouration to match their new surroundings.

Diet

Roktopi eat crabs, molluscs, and small fish. They can deliver potent venom, which causes motor paralysis and then tears the immobilized prey apart with its beak.

Behavior

Roktopi do not surface often, due to buoyancy issues, and prefer to lie flat on the seabed, pretending to be a pile of small rocks. When threatened, they may spray a jet of rocks, which blinds and confuses the aggressor, while roktopus makes its escape. When more aggressively attacked, the animal may separate a tentacle or two, which being rich in nervous tissue, continue to crawl along the seabed, deflecting the predator's attention from the remainder of the roktopus.

If there is no alternative, as when babies are threatened, roktopus can be an enthusiastic fighter, whomping opponents with all eight rock-encrusted tentacles. The well-defended roktopus is rarely hurt in such encounters, but may have to hole up for a few days after battle to regrow dislodged rocks.

Reproduction

The female roktopus lays approximately 100 eggs, attaching them to the walls of a sheltered cave. The babies are rockless when hatched, and are very vulnerable during infancy and the mother protects them for at least one month, when rocks begin to form. Even then, the infant roktopi provide a tasty, crunchy snack for predators, and many will be eaten in the first months of life.

Status

Like all newly discovered creatures of the Snugglays and surrounding waters, roktopi are protected and unauthorized removal of these animals, or of the gems which litter their environment, is strictly forbidden.

Department Of Defensive Operations (DODO) File
Wildlife of the Snugglay Islands
0003: *Scrab*
Kingdom: *Animalia;* Phylum: *Arthropoda*

Habitat

Scrabs are found only on the Hebridean Islands of Great and Little Snugglay. These unusual arthropods live at the shoreline, and can be found foraging in rock pools at low tide, or resting in temporary burrows dug in the sand or shale in the shelter of boulders.

Characteristics

Adult scrabs are approximately (3 inches) in length, with a bright green chiton carapace. The body is roughly cello-shaped, with thoracic and abdominal segments and a "waist" between them. Each of these two segments has six thin legs (twelve in total). The male scrab body is smooth, while the backs of females have twelve to fifteen white, dome-shaped "baby-cases." The head is wide and flat, with two pincers projecting from either side of a wide, horny, mouth, and two eyes attached to vertical eyestalks, which may be pulled close to the head for protection. The abdomen ends in a stinger, which in adults is approximately 2.5 cm (1 inch) long. Scrab venom contains bustulin, a relative of the bee venom protein melittin. If injected into the bloodstream, bustulin inserts into cell membranes and self-assembles into a protein pore, which allows rapid influx of water leading to cell lysis. In humans a scrab sting results in pain and inflammation affecting an area about (2 inches) in diameter for approximately one hour.

Diet

Most scrabs will eat anything that moves and is smaller than they are. Diet is typically small fish, insects and crustaceans. They will also feast in large numbers on carrion, such as a fish carcass.

Behavior

Favorite hunting times of the scrab are the morning and evening low tides. The pincers are used to shred food items too large to be swallowed whole. During high tides and in strong sunlight the animals burrow in the sand above the tidemark. Scrabs are non-aggressive and their response to threat is defensive, typically burrowing deep into sand or shale or taking refuge in rocky crevices. If forced to attack, the stinger delivers a warning, rather than serious injury, allowing the scrab to scuttle to safety while the aggressor reacts in surprise.

Reproduction

The scrab ovary is a thin layer directly beneath the carapace, and eggs are deposited directly up into the baby-cases. For the first three weeks, the young develop within these cases. After that they are able to roll back the skin, leaving the mother to crawl around in the open, and then crawl back in for protection.

Predators

Scrabs are a favorite delicacy of both rokchiks and regales.

Status

Like all newly discovered creatures of the Snugglays, the scrab is protected and removal of adults or babies is strictly forbidden.

Department Of Defensive Operations (DODO) File
Wildlife of the Snugglay Islands
0004: *Rokchik*
Kingdom: *Animalia;* Phylum: *Chordata*

Habitat

Rokchik is found only on the Hebridean islands of Great and Little Snugglay. These birds live in colonies in the numerous caves, which pepper the islands' chalk and quartz cliffs.

Characteristics

Calcium carbonate rocks at the ends of its feathers distinguish rokchik. Sodium Carbonate and Calcium Chloride, secreted separately from ducts co-localized in the skin, react to form the Calcium Carbonate "rocks" which remain anchored to the ducts:

$$Na2CO3 + CaCL2 = 2NaCl + CaCO3$$

Adult birds are typically gray and white, with blue, green, yellow and pink markings, which reflect the veins of quartz in the cliffs and assist with camouflage. When full grown, the birds are approximately (18 inches) long with fat, curved, blue beaks and large blue feet with three long front toes and one short back toe.

Diet

Rokchiks mainly eat fish, as well as shore-living insects, crustaceans, berries and grubs.

Behavior

When fully rock-encrusted, the rokchik is flightless, though agile, preferring to waddle around the shoreline, snacking. In water, the birds are strong swimmers and proficient divers; the large fat beak is especially adapted for catching fish.

Rokchik is not aggressive, however if attacked, and especially when babies are threatened, the birds are formidable opponents, using the rock-heavy wings to "whomp" would-be predators to devastating effect, whilst simultaneously jabbing with the curved, razor-sharp beak. Rokchiks live and fight communally and will fiercely defend their brethren, as well as their young. This community ethic, in addition to their daunting natural defenses, makes rokchik colonies very secure. In extreme situations, they are able to release the rocks from their feathers, and may beat the wings vigorously, creating a "rock storm." Post rock-release, the lightened rokchik can exercise the power of flight and make its escape while the aggressor reels in confusion, battered and blinded by dust. However, rokchik will never abandon dependent young, and in this situation will fight to the death.

Reproduction

Rokchiks mate for life and the female lays a single egg per year, in early March. The chicks hatch after one month's gestation, and are born fluffy, white, and devoid of rocks, which begin to appear after another month. The parents take turns guarding the nest and foraging for food. More than one rokchik family may share a cave and childcare duties.

When rocks begin to grow, the chicks venture out from the caves, and can be seen waddling on shore in groups, under proud parental guidance. They reach maturity in late summer, and produce their own first eggs the following spring.

Status

Like all newly discovered creatures of the Snugglays, rokchik is protected and removal of birds, chicks or eggs is strictly forbidden.

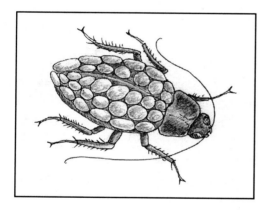

Department Of Defensive Operations (DODO) File Wildlife of the Snugglay Islands
0005: *Rokroach*
Kingdom: *Animalia;* Phylum: *Arthropoda*

Habitat

Rokroaches are found only on the Hebridean islands of Great and Little Snugglay, where they nest close to shore in complicated, calcium carbonate towers built from the rocks their bodies produce. The towers are easily mistaken for the islands' natural geology.

Characteristics

Rokroach is a six-legged, hard-shelled, non-flying beetle, between (1 - 2 inches) in length, whose carapace is covered in tiny calcium carbonate rocks. Ducts using an adaptation common to many of the islands' indigenous wildlife produce these rocks:

$$Na_2CO_3 + CaCL_2 = 2NaCl + CaCO_3$$

The rocks are grayish-white or black, and blend perfectly with the rock and shale of the Snugglay shoreline.

Diet

Rokroach feeds on vegetation: shoots, fruits and leaves.

Behavior

Rokroaches are active outside their towers during the dawn and twilight hours, when they collect vegetable material that they carry back to the tower. Although well camouflaged they are extremely nervous when disturbed and become frantic and disorganized. In this state they are easy prey for many island animals. Fortunately, they breed prolifically, so that their numbers are maintained.

Reproduction

Within each tower, eggs are laid by a single Queen, and the remainder of the rokroaches care for the eggs and larvae or forage outside for food.

Predators

Most island animals, except those that are strictly herbivorous, will eat rokroaches, which are particularly sought after because of their crunchy coat and juicy interior. It is possible that some of the native island people also snack on these insects occasionally.

Status

Like all newly discovered creatures of the Snugglays, rokroach is a protected species and removal of insects or eggs, or disturbance to their habitat is strictly forbidden.

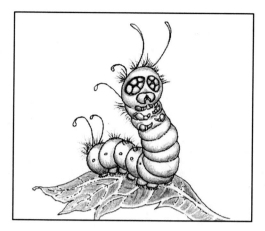

Department Of Defensive Operations (DODO) File
Wildlife of the Snugglay Islands
0006: *Acid Shooter*
Kingdom: *Animalia;* **Phylum:** *Arthropoda*

Habitat

The acid shooter, or acid poop-shooting caterpillar, is found only on the Hebridean Islands of Great and Little Snugglay.

Characteristics

A full-grown acid shooter is green, (3-4 inches) long and (.5 inch) in diameter, with tubular, segmented bodies that bristle with sensory hairs. They have three pairs of true legs that are used mainly for grasping food items on the front three segments of their bodies, and six additional pairs of prolegs, which develop into the legs of the adult insect. They advance with a surging, propulsive motion, in which the rear segments contract and push forward the front segments, which in turn contract and pull the rear ones. Although there are six eyes on each side of the head, vision is poor and most spatial information is gained via the sensory hairs. The mouth parts, or mandibles, are hard and sharp, well suited for chewing the tough leaves of the mangroid tree, and behind the mandibles are the spinnerets, which eject the liquid silk that will harden into the pupa, or chrysalis, when it is time for metamorphosis.

Diet

Acid shooters eat leaves and fruit of many varieties, with particular fondness for mangroid, tripodecon and thornego plants.

Behavior

Acid shooters are inoffensive lepidopterons, which exist only to eat, grow and pupate. Their intestines secrete pooptic acid, which allows them to digest efficiently their high cellulose plant diet. Each day they eat several times their own weight, and expel around twenty semi-liquid pellets of acidic waste matter. Raising their tails, they shoot the pellets for a distance of up to (1 foot). The gelatinous, corrosive slime digests and liquefies leaves and other plant parts with which it comes into contact, producing a soup with a now neutral pH, which provides dietary support for the adult life-stage, the pooptic putterfly (see life cycle).

Life Cycle

The acid shooter maintains caterpillar form for most of its life, spending at least twelve months in this stage. It pupates and undergoes metamorphosis over a one-month period, emerging as the fantastically beautiful pooptic putterfly, a delicate insect with gauzy, iridescent, rainbow colored wings. The pooptic putterfly feeds only on vegetable matter that has been predigested by pooptic acid expelled from the acid shooter's pooptic gland. This is the only known example in the Animal Kingdom of an adult life-stage depending absolutely for sustenance on the juvenile. The pooptic putterfly lives for only two weeks, its primary activities being eating and depositing eggs on the undersides of mangroid leaves. Early caterpillars emerge after a further two weeks gestation and grow to full size within one month.

Predators

Acid shooters and their eggs are a preferred delicacy of the rokchik and the reagle. The acid contained within their bodies does not deter the birds, but does limit consumption to two or three caterpillars per meal, after which violent indigestion inevitably ensues. The diners always return for more, appearing unable to resist the spicy larvae, and a working hypothesis of physiological addiction is currently being investigated.

Status

Acid shooters, pooptic putterflies and their eggs are protected species and interference with them or their habitat carries serious penalties.

Department Of Defensive Operations (DODO) File
Wildlife of the Snugglay Islands
0007: *Sleepypotamus*
Kingdom: *Animalia;* Phylum: *Chordata*

Habitat

Planet Earth boasts a single known colony of sleepypotami, on the slopes and caves of Ben Slumber on the Hebridean Island of Little Snugglay. The Ben overhangs Loch Snooze, which provides these engaging mammals with essential opportunities to play, swim and fish.

Characteristics

An adult sleepypotamus weighs between (100 and 200 lbs) and is covered in dense, soft, pink or lavender fur. The face is similar to that of a koala. They have four short legs and a stubby tail. Due to a complicated joint arrangement, they are able to flatten their bodies completely when in repose, which allows them to self-conceal in the absence of cover. The evolutionary advantage of this adaptation is unknown, since they appear to face no danger from aggressors in their natural habitat. Sleepypotami are known to be highly intelligent, and, in the opinions of some experts, may rival humans in this respect.

Diet

Sleepypotami feed on flowers, berries and fish.

Behavior

These engaging mammals divide their time between hunting for fish, basking on the grass among the wildflowers, where they are easily mistaken for patches of mountain heather, and rolling down the hill at speed until they bounce off the ridge over Loch Snooze and splash into the water. They accompany this activity with characteristic cries of Wheep! Whaa! and Whoo! In inclement weather they shelter in the deep caves that pock the mountainside.

Family Life

Sleepypotami mate for life, and the group shares collective responsibility for the young. Orphaned babies are cared for and loved to the same degree as those with living parents. They are believed to share complicated rituals and ceremonies, however these have not been observed in detail and are poorly understood.

Predators

None known.

Status

Sleepypotami are very strictly protected, and interference with them or their habitat carries serious penalties.

Department Of Defensive Operations (DODO) File
Wildlife of the Snugglay Islands
0008: *Thornego Plant*
Kingdom: *Plantae;* **Division:** *Anthrophyta*

Habitat

The Thornego plant is found in large numbers on the Hebridean islands of Great and Little Snugglay.

Characteristics

This unusual flowering plant grows in clusters or groves. The central woody stem is typically (2 feet tall) but heights of up to (5 feet) have been documented. Multiple branches grow from the central stem. Leaves are flat, arrow shaped, and bright green and flowers small and rose-colored with a patina of gold. The flowering period is brief—approximately two weeks in early May—and is followed by fruiting. The soft fruits, or seedpods, are initially an intense pink color and covered with sharp, curved spikes about (2 inches) long. They grow to the size and shape of a grapefruit. Immature seeds are green and covered with a slime that is intensely irritating to mammalian skin, resulting in a rash of painful raised white blisters, which resolve after one to two weeks. When ripe the pods and seeds are golden and the seeds are dry and non-irritant. As the pods mature they swell around the curved spikes until the rind is punctured and the golden seeds spill out to propagate this fascinating species.

Possible Medicinal Uses

Like many newly discovered island species, thornego plants may have medicinal properties. There is some evidence that local people use the ripe seeds to treat minor illnesses, and investigators, before strict control on use of the seeds was implemented, reported a feeling of intense well-being and enhanced physical and mental abilities after ingesting them. It is also rumored that native Hebrideans use a dilute solution of immature seed extract to treat various skin complaints and retard the formation of wrinkles. Government limits on harvesting of wild thornego seeds now limits the pace of investigation, and a project to farm the plants at the Great Snugglay DODO compound is in progress.

Threats to Survival

Ripe thornego seeds are a prized food item among island wildlife, notably the sleepypotami, which make several excursions per year from their mountain to collect them, however they never harvest more than ten percent of available seeds. Some observers postulate that the potami actively protect the thornego plant, removing caterpillars and damaged leaves.

Acid shooting caterpillars will eat thornego leaves, but prefer mangroids.

None of the animals or insects indigenous to the islands damages plant structure or root system.

Status

Thornegos are strictly protected and removal of plants, flowers, seeds or fruit from the islands is forbidden by law.

Department Of Defensive Operations (DODO) File
Wildlife of the Snugglay Islands
0009: *Frokhoppers*
Kingdom: *Animalia;* Phylum: *Chordata*

Habitat

These small amphibians are found only on the Hebridean islands of Great and Little Snugglay, where they inhabit ponds and swamps that have a covering of chillypads.

Characteristics

Adult Frokhoppers are (1-2 inches) long and bright green. In health the animals are completely covered with small rocks. Sodium Carbonate and Calcium Chloride, secreted separately from ducts co-localized in the skin, react to form the Calcium Carbonate "rocks" which remain anchored to the ducts:

$$Na_2CO_3 + CaCL_2 = 2NaCl + CaCO_3$$

The rocks are uniformly spherical and colored by green pigment secreted by the frokhopper, providing camouflage.

Diet

Frokhoppers use their long, tube-like tongues to ingest sugar- and protein-rich chillypad nectar. The tongue can also be unrolled rapidly to catch insects that venture near the pond surface, but chillypad nectar is the main food source.

Behavior

Frokhoppers live exclusively on the chillypad surface, where they can be heard croaking during the night hours. In daylight they typically crouch immobile on the pad surface, pretending to be hills of beans, unless roused to action by hovering insects.

Life Cycle and Symbiosis with Chillypads

Frokhoppers and chillypads are mutually dependent. The chillypad plant produces a natural refrigerant, which, if unopposed, would result in complete freezing of the pond environment and consequent failure of the plant's reproductive strategy. Frokhoppers and their tadpoles secrete a biological anti-freeze that keeps the pond water liquid at sub-zero temperatures and limits ice formation on the pads to a thin skin of crystals. In turn, frokhoppers depend on the cold generated by the chillypads for survival. The threat of warmth to the animal is poorly understood. The current working hypothesis is that in warmer temperatures various critical biochemical pathways proceed too rapidly resulting in uncontrolled cell division as well as hyperthermia.

Frokhopper spawn is deposited on the chillypad surface, from where it drips through pores in the leaf to collect in pouches below the water level where the tadpoles develop. As the young grow, the pouches swell until they are punctured by curved spikes that depend from the pad's underside, releasing the tadpoles that become free-swimming but remain associated with the lower surface of the chillypad, from which they derive sustenance while metamorphosing into adult frokhoppers. Back and front legs develop in sequence, then the tail shrinks, and when it is completely gone the frokhopper climbs over the chillypad rim to join its family in the basin.

The chillypad leaves block sunlight in the pond, preventing colonization by other potentially predatory creatures, thus protecting both the plants and their companions. Unlike other amphibian species, frokhopper tadpoles do not require sunlight and it is believed that they depend on darkness to develop.

Possible Medicinal and Commercial Uses

Frokhopper anti-freeze may have important medicinal and other applications, and is under investigation by DODO scientists.

Predators and Threats to Survival

Frokhoppers provide an occasional tasty treat for island birds, but are well camouflaged by their rock covering and usually overlooked. Their frigid environment suppresses their scent, which aids in their concealment. The main threat to survival of these interesting amphibians is their absolute dependence on the delicate symbiosis between themselves and the chillypads. Any imbalance in this intricate ecosystem would present a serious risk to both species.

Status

Frokhoppers are strictly protected and removal of adults, tadpoles or spawn, or interference with their habitat, is forbidden by law.

Department Of Defensive Operations (DODO) File
Wildlife of the Snugglay Islands
0010: *Chillypad*
Kingdom: *Plantae;* Phylum: *Magniolophyta*

Habitat

Chillypads are found only on the Hebridean islands of Great and Little Snugglay, where they grow on ponds and swamps that are populated by frokhoppers.

Characteristics

The chillypad leaf can be several feet in diameter and is circular with a low rim that forms a shallow basin that prevents frokhoppers from slipping off. The leaf is pocked with small holes leading to underwater "nursery-pouches," where frokhopper eggs are deposited and develop. The underside of the pad is also densely armored with curved, two-inch long spikes, which serve two purposes: they discourage island animals from eating the plants, and also rupture the nursery-pouches when the frokhopper tadpoles are large enough for release, thus ensuring adequate supply of the anti-freeze which maintains the pond in liquid state. The topside of the chillypad is usually coated with a thin layer of snow and ice crystals.

Chillypad flowers are white, fluffy, about the size of a soccer ball, and produce fructose- and protein- rich nectar that is the frokhoppers' main food source.

Possible Medicinal and Commercial uses

Chillypad refrigerant may have important uses in medicine, food preservation and transport, and many other enterprises and is the subject of intense research effort at the DODO.

Life Cycle and Symbiosis with Frokhoppers

Chillypads are flowering plants that depend on pollination by frokhoppers for successful reproduction. The amphibians sit within the fluffy white flowers, drinking nectar through their long, flexible, tube-tongues and becoming coated with pollen, which they transport to the flowers of other chillypads. In return, chillypads provide frokhoppers with a home, food, and protection from predators and their tendency to hyperthermia. The entire arrangement is dependent on the balance between frokhopper anti-freeze and chillypad refrigerant.

Predators and Threats to Survival

Chillypad spikes discourage island animals from eating them, and the main threat to survival of the species is the delicacy of their symbiotic relationship with the frokhoppers. Any disturbance to the balance of this intricate ecosystem presents a serious risk to the survival of both.

Status

Chillypads are strictly protected and removal of or damage to the plants is strictly forbidden by law.

Department Of Defensive Operations (DODO) File
Wildlife of the Snugglay Islands
0010: *Reagle*
Kingdom: *Animalia;* Phylum: *Chordata*

Habitat

The reagle is found only on the Hebridean islands of Great and Little Snugglay. These birds nest in solitary eyries built high on cliffs and crags.

Characteristics

These large, fully-flighted birds have a wingspan of approximately (12 feet) and are fledged with green and purple feathers. The beak and talons are golden yellow and they have a circular crest, or crown, of golden yellow spikes, approximately (6 inches) long. This circlet of spikes appears to be important for their direction and spatial sense and it is believed that they possess a primitive form of radar.

Diet

The reagle is the Snugglay's top predator and is exclusively carnivorous. Diet is mainly fish and small mammals. Large reagles have been known to carry off fully grown seals.

Behavior

When not caring for chicks, reagles rest quietly except when hunting. They hunt in isolation, swooping down to grasp their prey in beak or talons.

Reproduction

Reagles mate for life and lay four or five eggs per clutch in early spring. Chicks hatch within four weeks and are white and fluffy. Adult purple and green feathers grow in within about six months. The nesting pair takes turns guarding the young and foraging for food for the chicks.

Status

Like all newly discovered creatures of the Snugglays, reagles are protected and removal of birds, chicks or eggs is strictly forbidden.

A word about *A Word with You Press, Publishers and Purveyors of Fine Stories.*

In addition to being a publishing house, *A Word with You Press* is a playful, passionate, and prolific consortium of writers connected by our collective love of the written word. We are, as well, devoted readers, drawn to the notion that there is nothing more beautiful or powerful than a well-told story.

www.awordwithyoupress.com is the planet we inhabit in cyberspace, although writers lucky enough to live in the San Diego area are also welcome at our clubhouse headquarters in Oceanside, California, at 802 South Tremont Street. We offer multiple daily posts on our home-page blog, as well as book reviews, tips on writing more effectively, notices of writing and publishing events held around the country, a weekly cartoon by award-winning cartoonist Ruth Joyce, and—our most popular feature—regular writing competitions to encourage and inspire writers to stretch their imaginations.

We're not just for writers, though—we also have a place for artists, *The Artist Alcove,* especially for visual artists, with contests, interviews, and online galleries exhibiting featured artists' work, which can be purchased directly from the site.

Finally, we realize that great writers and artists don't just happen. They are nurtured, inspired, and mentored. They are the lucky few who discover that art is not a diversion or distraction from everyday life; rather, art is an essential expression of the human spirit. *A Word with You Press* is so profoundly committed to this belief that we have founded a non-profit organization, *Kid Expression,* to provide free mentoring to children to help them find their inner artists and give them the tools to express themselves beautifully through the written word.

Our *Kid Expression* workshop, led by volunteer mentors, combines one-on-one instruction with group activities. To honor their accomplishments, each child who completes the workshop is rewarded with a debut book-signing event, where they can see their own work in print as part of an anthology published by *A Word with You Press.* To learn more, visit www.kidxpress.us.

About the Author

Isabelle Rooney-Freedman grew up on the West Coast of Scotland and has worked as a doctor and scientist in Britain, Switzerland and the USA. She is married to Pulitzer Prize-winning writer Jonathan Freedman. They live with their children, Viva and Lincoln, in a strange urban forest in North California with an assortment of small mammals, amphibians and invertebrates. *Angus MacDream and the Roktopus Rogue* is her first book in print. She has written another book, *Morag's Monsters*, for Viva, and hopes that it, too, may one day be published.

About the Artist

Teri Rider's love of art began at an early age and evolved into a business she is passionate about. Her career began as a fine artist, selling her work in galleries and taking a few illustration jobs along the way. She discovered her  love of publishing when she began illustrating for a well-known publisher of special education material, and authored, illustrated and collaborated on more than 100 books during her employment there. She now owns her own graphic design studio where she offers services to authors as they self-publish their works. Her primary interests are illustrating children's and young adult books and book design for all genre.

She lives in Vista, California with her husband and menagerie of dogs, cats and exotic birds. Contact her at teririder.com.

9 780984 306435